Haunted Visions

Where Darkness Reigns

Grace's Story

Book 5

By: Mary Reason Theriot

Dedication

Without the love and support of my family and friends, I would not have pursued this new path in life. I would especially like to thank those that have proofread copy after copy, to give me their honest opinion of the books.

Theresa, thank you so much for your continued encouragement. Without you, some of the characters would not have "come to life."

To my wonderful husband Malwen, your continued love and support mean the world to me. I don't know what I would do without you in my life. One of these nights I'm sure you will be able to sleep with both eyes closed. Eventually, I should run out of ideas… or maybe not. These books wouldn't be what they are without you pushing me forward.

To Don Reason and Malcolm "Phil" Theriot for sharing your knowledge and experience of Law Enforcement protocol.

To my fans, I would like to offer a special thank you for your continued support.

Acknowledgement

To Adele Hartman for not only keeping the website current with the constant change of information, but also with the proofreading and editorial suggestions. No one could ask for a better friend and confidant.

To Amy Brown Sosa, thank you for allowing me to toss around different menu ideas with you.

Wow Wee Dipping Sauce can be purchased at www.wowweedippingsauce.com

Resa's BBQ Shrimp by Resa Theriot

As a special thank you for purchasing this book, I have included my daughter's BBQ shrimp recipe. For this and other recipes she has please visit www.maryreasontheriot.me.

Beazell's Cajun Seasoning can be purchased at www.beazells.com. The recipe for Beazell's Bloody Mary can also be found on their website.

DAT Sauce can be contacted at www.facebook.com/dat.sauce.7 or dat.sauce@yahoo.com

1 pound of shrimp

One Lemon

3 cloves garlic, minced   0

1 stick butter

1 tablespoon Worcestershire sauce

1/4 onion, chopped

Beazell's Cajun Seasoning

Dash of DAT Sauce

You can either use the headless, head on or already peeled and deveined shrimp. When using the peeled and deveined shrimp cooking time is much faster.

Melt butter and add garlic, Worcestershire sauce, DAT sauce, and onion.

Arrange shrimp in a glass baking dish. Pour butter mixture over shrimp.

Sprinkle Beazell's liberally over the shrimp, making sure to turn and sprinkle the other side as well.

Slice lemon and place lemon slices over shrimp.

Bake in a 400 degree oven for 20 minutes or until shrimp are done. Watch carefully. If you overcook the shell on shrimp, it will be harder to peel shrimp.

We love to have fresh French bread on the side with this dish, that way you can soak up all the butter the shrimp cooked in with the French bread.

Also Available by Mary Reason Theriot:

The Hideaway

The Traveler

Dr. Frankenstein

Above Suspicion

Horror in the Night

Deadly Seduction

Echoes on the Bayou

Seven Deadly Sins

A Kiss So Deadly

Deadly Combination

CarnEvil of Souls

Seduced by Voodoo

www.maryreasontheriot.com

Prologue

He hid in the safety of the shadows. The darkness of the night was his ally, his best friend and his confidant. He was not afraid of the dark. He actually thrived in the darkness. He found safety in the shadows. In the shadows, he could watch and wait.

She never had a chance to scream before the arms reached out from the alley and dragged her into the darkness. He had been waiting and watching. She was too stunned to react at first. By the time she could utter a scream, the cold edge of the blade cut into her tender flesh.

As with each kill, once he was at home, he placed the precious contents he'd carefully collected into their respective jars. Each jar was filled with a liquid that forever preserved his treasures. After meticulously completing the task, he opened the hidden panel in the wall of his private sanctuary and placed the newly acquired trophies on the shelf. It was not until after this ritual was performed that he surrendered to the voices raging inside of his head.

Before leaving his private sanctuary, he made sure the lock was securely latched. It wasn't until he knew that his mementos were locked away that he could leave this room. Even after this recent kill, the hunger ate away at him again; it had become almost insatiable lately. It was too soon to hunt again. He pled with the voices to stay silent for a little while before he went out once again.

They refused to be silent. He slammed his fist down on the desk and smashed the glass containing his water. He inadvertently cut himself. He stood there and just watched as the blood flowed down his hand. It was thick and slowly congealing.

The voices mocked and laughed at him more. He trembled with hatred as he begged the voices to be silent. Suddenly, he caught a glimpse of himself in the mirror across the room. His image sent a flood of memories through his mind, memories that he wished he could have long ago forgotten.

The ornate mirror hanging on the wall was one of his mother's most cherished possessions. It hung in this room like a shrine to her. Although tarnished and faded from years of neglect, it still remained here in the house.

He backed away from the mirror as the image of his mother moved in behind him. Even after death, she still walked these halls. The devil himself didn't want his mother. He ran his hands through his hair as he recalled her lectures over the years. Even though the mirror had been one of her most prized possessions, she informed him it was to remind both of them of the evils of vanity.

Still, he couldn't help but marvel at his reflection. Women often commented on just how mesmerizing his eyes were and how they could lure them into doing whatever he desired.

He thought he could destroy his mother's voice forever by removing her tongue, but it did nothing to silence her. Worse, it came back from the grave to torment him. Of all the ghosts who visited him, she was the most frequent. She hounded him day and night; he could not walk away from her constant nagging.

Her voice was as clear today as it had been the day she died. It was as if she was right here beside him, vehemently preaching to him about how wicked girls were and how dirty little boys were. One day, she caught him touching himself, and he could still feel the switch hitting him, leaving welts upon his tender flesh, whenever he thought of touching himself.

Growing up, not a single day went by that she didn't comment on her feelings of disappointment in him and his uselessness. The hate, anger and disappointment that echoed in her voice whenever she talked to or about anyone was deeply ingrained in him. It was an intrinsic part of his psyche. She was the whole reason he was this way.

Suddenly, the image staring back at him in the mirror was a monster, the monster she created. She made it impossible for him to make any friends. He grew up isolated, only having her for companionship. He didn't know how to act in front of other children. He didn't know how to talk to a girl and shied away whenever one smiled at him.

His teachers always thought he was overly shy, but he had been scared they would demean him just like his mother. His fear of being belittled in front of others forced him to sit there quietly. She raised him not to talk unless he had permission. She believed children should not be seen nor heard from unless necessary.

His father walked out on his mother before his birth. She always blamed him for his father walking out on them, but maybe he didn't like her demeanor. Whenever he mentioned his father, he received an unmerciful beating for whatever reason. He quickly learned never to bring up his father, ever.

He had hoped that killing his mother and cutting out her tongue would silence her, but it did not. It was as if her death restored her eyes and her tongue. The women reminded him of his mother, so he purposefully removed their eyes and tongue. He kept the eyes as his mementos. He kept them tucked away from his mother's view. His mother said eyes were the windows to the soul, but these women were like his mother, soulless bitches who deserved to die. Taking their eyes removed their evil souls and preserving their eyes meant that he could keep their souls from haunting his every movement.

He was becoming much more efficient in removing the eyes. Honing his skill with each kill. If only he could silence his mother's voice in his head; then perhaps he could stop killing.

His mind drifted towards the woman he met the other day at church. He had never laid eyes on anyone that lovely. He instantly knew she was someone special. She didn't even resemble his mother. Just seeing the woman sent a never felt before feeling rushing through him. He couldn't help but wonder if she could be the one to silence his mother's voice. Maybe through her, he would find true love. He must make her his.

His mother must have realized he was thinking of her once again because he heard her voice raging through his mind about how wicked women were. He picked up his knife and surveyed it. He felt the sharp blade. The knife brought him some peace from his mother's incessant nagging. She may have stopped her nagging, but he still felt her in his mind. Silence, all he wished was to finally make her silent.

Chapter 1

Renee Breaux headed out to I-10. She had a long drive ahead of her, but was ready to get home. Her parents would rather she made this drive during the day, but she preferred to drive at night when the roads were quiet. She had made this drive many times in the past and knew the roads like the back of her hand.

Before getting on the interstate, she stopped and bought a venti white chocolate caramel latte for a caffeine rush and turned up the radio. She was ready for a break and some of her mom's cooking. Midterms had been harder this year, and she needed some time to unwind before the spring semester started.

Earlier, she had packed the Christmas gifts and her luggage in the car. By the time her parents woke up in the morning, she should be home. As she made her way onto the Pontchartrain Causeway, her car sputtered just before it died. She let out moan as she tried to start it up once again. "Great, this is all I need." She had told her dad that the car had been acting up, and he promised to check it as soon as she got home. Now she wished she had taken the time to get it checked before leaving. She honestly did not think it would break down on her.

It was just her luck; there wasn't another car around. She hated having to call a tow truck and delay her trip to see her parents. As she picked up her cell phone to locate a tow truck company, she saw a pair of headlights heading her way. Maybe she would get lucky, and it was a state trooper making rounds.

As the car approached, she noticed that it was a taxi driver instead of a cop. Standing at the rear of her vehicle, she waved her hands in the air, hoping he saw her in the darkness of the night.

Renee never noticed the knife in his hand. All she felt was the searing pain as he slit her throat. She was dead before she hit the ground.

***

With expert precision, he swiftly removed her eyes and tongue and placed them carefully in the container he brought with him. Once home, he would store them.

Not wanting to spend any more time near the scene, he shoved the body under the car and left the scene. As he drove off, he still couldn't believe how quiet the Pontchartrain Causeway was tonight. This kill was meant to be.

Chapter 2

Detective Grace Hutcherson, Hutch to most, tried to convince her boyfriend, Mike, into joining her on a morning run, but he laughed at her. He informed her she was crazy if she thought he would get out of bed to sweat. He even suggested that she come back to bed, and he would give her a personal workout. While the offer was tempting, if she wanted to keep her body fit and toned, she had to stick to her routine and not miss too many days. She tried to run every day, but her line of work didn't always make that possible, so she must take advantage of the days when she could run outside. Today was one of those days, so she left the apartment at five o'clock for her morning run.

Typically, her morning run lasted forty-five minutes. During those forty-five minutes, she prepared herself for the day ahead. Most of her days were hectic and nerve-racking. The first mile of the run was her warm up, and it usually took her that long to find her rhythm. She preferred jogging here instead of on the River Walk; she enjoyed the smells that emitted from the local businesses. There was something relaxing to her as she took in the smell of the coffee, the beignets being cooked and the murky water of the Mississippi River.

This morning she wore her white nylon shorts and a bright pink tank top, both showed off her nicely tanned body. She checked the weather before heading out this morning. Today would be in the high eighties, but by tomorrow, a cold front would be moving in, and the temperatures would once again drop. Only in Louisiana could it be eighty degrees one minute and then drop fifty degrees before the sun went down.

Her movements were always graceful and smooth when she ran. It was quiet out this morning. She took the time to enjoy the solitude. As she made it to her halfway point, dawn was breaking. Eager to get back home to see Mike, she picked up her pace. Perhaps he was still up to a little loving before heading to work. When she made it back home, the coffee should be finished. She loved walking into the house and smelling the aroma of freshly brewed coffee.

The wind picked up from the river. The breeze was more than welcome. The run helped her work up a good sweat this morning. She needed to work off the extra calories from last night's meal, along with the dessert. The creamy deliciousness of the bread pudding with amaretto sauce was worth it though.

It was muggier than normal this morning. As much as she loved living in Louisiana, there was something wrong with wearing shorts for Christmas. Come summer, the oppressive heat was always miserable. With winter here, you never knew if you would be bundled up or wearing shorts. Some days it would be bitterly cold when you woke up and by the afternoon you wished for the cold once more.

***

Hutch felt the vision closing in on her while in the shower. She closed her eyes tightly and then opened them once more, hoping the image disappeared, but the apparition was still standing in front of her, just standing there. When she first saw the spirit, it scared her more than any of the other visions. This woman standing in front of her was missing her eyes and more than likely her tongue. She didn't want to stare too long, but the woman appeared to have blood streaking down her cheeks to her chin.

Once again, Hutch cursed the vampire they'd killed. Ever since running into him at the carnival, it seemed that he'd opened a door she would prefer to have left closed. Unlike her other family members who had this gift, she had limited capabilities of her family's gift. In the past, Hutch could only read a scene after someone died there, depending on the energy left behind by the death. Ever since her run in with the vampire and the carnival, her gift was more prominent. It was like the floodgates opened and all hope of normalcy left with that opening. Now, it seemed as if ghosts sought her out, asking for her help in finding peace so they could move on.

From the looks of the latest ghost, she appeared to be the victim of a vicious murder. A shudder wracked through Hutch's body as she envisioned what this poor woman went through in death. Since the woman couldn't talk, Hutch had no idea when she died or even who did this to her. She was unsure if the murder happened recently or years ago. By the looks of her outfit, the woman was killed recently though. Before Hutch could ask the woman any questions, she disappeared as quickly as she appeared.

She let out a sigh. She would have to check the latest missing persons' reports filed. This new gift was turning into a curse. Some days all she saw was a faint coloration in the air, but other days she saw the dead as if they were standing right next to her.

When this first happened, the hair on her body would stand on end, but now, she was becoming used to it. When the visions of the past mingled with those of the recently departed, it caused her problems. Those killed decades or centuries ago were much harder to help move on. Some nights her dreams took her to times and places completely unknown to her.

Chapter 3

Detective Paul Ledet thought he was dreaming when the phone rang. As he went to answer the phone, he glanced over at the alarm clock and saw it was barely three a.m. He groaned. A call this early in the morning meant a homicide. "Ledet speaking."

He listened as the dispatcher relayed the information. "I'm on my way."

As he jumped out of bed, he called his partner, Detective Max Bryant, "Our killer struck again. He left the body shoved under a car on the Pontchartrain Causeway."

Detective Bryant stated, "I'll be waiting outside for you."

Ledet didn't even bother jumping in the shower. He grabbed the outfit he'd taken off a few short hours ago and headed right back out the door. It was going to be one of those days. He dreaded that he was about to ruin a family's Christmas.

After he had picked up Bryant, they headed straight to the crime scene. By the time they arrived, the scene was in complete chaos. The media had learned about the murder and were at the scene. There were also more than a dozen police cruisers, and several police officers were trying to keep everyone away from the scene.

As he walked to the car, he noticed that the body was still under the car. One of the younger officers working the perimeters replied, "Sir, Dr. Ortego just called to say he is almost here. He is having a hard time getting the van around all the media."

Bryant exclaimed, "Get these media vans out of the way so that the crime scene vans can get in here. Let's not keep Dr. Ortego waiting."

It took ten minutes to get the media to move further away from the scene so that Dr. Ortego and the crime scene techs could get in with their vans.

As Ledet spoke to the responding officer, he could tell this was his first homicide. The poor guy had never seen this amount of carnage before. He thought when he stopped behind the automobile he would be assisting a stranded motorist. At first, it appeared to be an abandoned car, but while radioing for a tow truck from his cruiser, a shape from under the car caught his attention. Upon closer inspection, he became disturbed by what he found.

"Sir, how could someone do that? Her eyes were removed."

This case would leave a permanent mark on the young rookie's mind. As Ledet looked at the body, he told the young rookie, "At least the killer slit her throat before removing her eyes. She was probably dead before she hit the ground."

Ledet hollered out to one of the crime scene techs, "Make sure you photograph the crime scene from every angle. We need accurate measurements on the position of the body. I want plenty of pictures. Don't worry about how many rolls of film you use, just get it done."

To the responding officer, he instructed, "Make sure you take plenty of notes on everything you saw before, during and after the discovery of the body. Don't leave anything out. No matter how insignificant it seems, it may prove to be vital evidence afterward."

Another crime scene tech was combing the area for evidence. Ledet instructed him, "I want you to catalog everything you take. Mark down everything in the immediate vicinity. Write down what type of debris you removed and where it was removed."

To everyone, he stated, "I want to be overly thorough with this crime scene. Take your time and be careful. I don't want anything missed. Understood?"

They chimed in unison, "Yes, sir."

He watched the flurry of activity around him. A set of tire tracks was found near the rear of the car. At least the responding officer had followed protocol and kept his eight foot distance from the car. They were able to get a few good pictures of the tread. Other than that, there wasn't sufficient evidence for them to go on.

As Dr. Ortego got out of his van, Ledet noticed how much he had aged recently. His hair started to gray and thin. He asked Ledet, "What have we got?"

"We have a dead body under the car. The body hasn't been moved. We wanted you to have a look first."

Dr. Ortego asked, "And you are sure it is your killer?"

Ledet nodded his head, "You can tell right away that her eyes are missing."

Dr. Ortego's assistants removed the body. "I will have the autopsy reports for you as soon as possible." He continued to bark orders to his personnel before leaving the scene.

By the time Ledet made it back to the office that afternoon, he had found the young woman's parents at his desk. Mr. Breaux looked at his wife, "Why don't you stay here? I can do this by myself."

She shook her head, "No, I want to do this with you."

Ledet asked, "Mrs. Breaux, are you sure about this? You don't want to remember your daughter like this."

She shook her head, "No, I must see her. I have to know it is her."

Ledet hated that they would spend their Christmas holiday identifying their daughter's body instead of celebrating the season with family.

Dr. Ortego met them in the reception area of the coroner's office. "Dr. Ortego, this is Mr. and Mrs. Breaux. Mr. and Mrs. Breaux this is the medical examiner, Dr. Ortego."

Dr. Ortego shook each of their hands, "I'm sorry we have to meet under such a somber occasion. If you would sign in please, I will wait for you in the back. Detective Ledet will bring you back when you are ready."

Before entering the morgue, Detective Ledet knocked on the door to let Dr. Ortego know that they were there. He opened the door, "You can come in. She is ready."

Ledet led them into the room. Inside the room stood a steel table with a sheet covering a prone figure. An involuntary shiver ran through Ledet's body. He despised this aspect of the job. The morgue was so cold and impersonal. The air smelled of chemicals and death. There was no possible way to bring comfort or to ease the pain of those left behind as they came to identify the body.

Mrs. Breaux moved towards the table in slow motion. Dr. Ortego pulled back the sheet. Mr. Breaux wrapped his arms around his wife as she took in a sudden breath. Her face turned white as a ghost just as her eyes rolled back, and her knees buckled.

Thankfully, Mr. Breaux had his arms around her just as she went to faint. Dr. Ortego rolled the wheelchair over to her. Detective Ledet helped Mr. Breaux settle her into the chair.

Dr. Ortego reached into his pocket and broke out the smelling salts. He waved it under her nose. She woke up suddenly and pushed his hand away from her, "I'm fine now."

Dr. Ortego asked, "Are you sure?"

She nodded her head, "Really, I am fine. I never expected that reaction, but it was more than I could take." She wiped the tears from her eyes "My poor baby. Do you know what happened to her?"

Detective Ledet put his hand on her shoulder, "Mrs. Breaux, please don't do this to yourself. She didn't suffer if that will help you, but as far as how she died, we needed to keep that to ourselves until the investigation is complete. I hope you understand that?"

She nodded in understanding, "I don't know what I will do without my baby." Great, heaving sobs shook her body. Dr. Ortego handed her a box of tissue from his desk as her husband took her in his arms.

He despised this part of the notification - the tears and the emotions. He was not good at providing comfort. Until they stopped this killer, there would be more notifications. This killer was just getting started.

Mr. Breaux applied a firm grasp to Ledet's shoulder, "Please find the monster that did this to my daughter. She didn't deserve to die this young and especially in this manner."

Ledet patted Mr. Breaux's back, "I promise I will do everything in my power to find the person responsible for your daughter's death."

Chapter 4

As he prepared for the Sunday service, his stomach tightened in anticipation. They were having a breakfast following this morning's sermon. Today was the day he would ask her out. She was all he thought about lately, and he finally gathered the courage to do this.

When he heard the announcement last week, he knew this was God's way of telling him it was time. He needed to seize the moment.

He arrived early and waited for her. His heart pounded as each person entered. Service was about to begin, and she hadn't arrived. Disappointment settled down deep inside of him as he realized she would not be coming. Just as he was about to give up all hope of her coming, she walked in the door, flushed.

He found this morning's sermon slow as he anxiously waited for the breakfast to begin. It seemed like an eternity passed before the priest said the final prayer. Not wanting to appear too anxious, he waited until she got up to leave, and he followed her. He said a little prayer that she was attending the breakfast.

His heart skipped a beat when he saw her follow the crowd into the hall. The aroma of pancakes, scrambled eggs, bacon and coffee filled the hall. As everyone stood in line for coffee, he moved to a back corner and watched her through veiled eyes.

It was the first time he'd seen her outside of the church; he found himself tongue-tied and unsure if he could approach her now. It was as if his feet were glued to the floor. He paid close attention to everything she did.

When he saw her alone at the coffee pot, he found the courage to approach her. This gave him the perfect opportunity to approach her. "Is the coffee any good?"

She took a timid sip and grimaced as she picked up another pack of sugar and cream. "It's a little bitter for my liking, but with enough sugar, I am sure it will be fine."

As he poured himself a cup of coffee, he caught a whiff of her. She smelled like a fresh summer morning. When he took a sip and grimaced, she gave him a smile that caused his heart to do somersaults. "I warned you."

He relaxed in her presence, "Yes, you did. I thought the coffee I made was strong, but this would surely keep you moving."

"I've noticed you in church. My name is Gabrielle Hanson."

He took her extended hand and felt a charge of electricity run through his body when their hands touched. Even her name was perfect. "It is a pleasure to meet you Gabrielle. Would you care to join me for breakfast?"

"I would like that very much." He took her elbow and walked her over to a table. There weren't too many people sitting at the table he chose. They had a chance to get to know each other a little better.

By the time breakfast was over, they had made plans to go out for dinner Friday night. On the drive home, his mother's incessant nagging couldn't bring down his mood. For once, he tuned her out and enjoyed his ride home. He could still smell Gabrielle's intoxicating perfume and the feel of her warm hand in his. Yes, he was glad he'd found the courage to ask her out. He couldn't wait until Friday night when he saw her again.

To keep the ghosts silent until then, there was one thing that he must do.

Chapter 5

Ledet woke up with a heavy sense of foreboding. They still had no good leads regarding the current murder case. How could someone get killed on the Pontchartrain Causeway and there not be any witnesses?

He had a bad feeling about this and wanted to review the file once more. The autopsy report should be done by now. He didn't want to miss a thing, so if that meant reviewing the information again he would.

As soon as he arrived, he saw the autopsy report on his desk. He told the receptionist, "I am going to grab a coffee and find a quiet spot to look over this file. Call me on my cell phone if you need me."

The local coffee shop should be quiet for another hour. As he entered, he confirmed his assumption. It was still too early for the morning rush. He ordered his beignets and his coffee and found a booth in the back corner to spread out the files.

Flipping open the manila file, pictures of the young woman greeted him. He shook his head in disgust. A maniac had cut short this poor young girl's life. The college student on her way home to see her parents had unfortunately broken down on the Pontchartrain Causeway. She probably thought a good Samaritan had stopped to help her. By the looks of the autopsy report, death came quickly. Her eyes and tongue were removed postmortem. The knife had a smooth edge, almost similar to something you would use to filet a fish. The wounds were neat with no hesitation marks.

The blade was about six or seven inches long and extremely sharp.

So far, she had no known enemies or a jealous boyfriend. It looked as if her death was simply the result of being in the wrong place at the wrong time. What twist of fate made this poor girl intersect with such evil? Was this written in the stars or just plain bad luck? Another thought crossed his mind, could this be premeditated? Did someone know she would be leaving to see her parents at this time? Did they rig her car to break down?

Ledet took a bite of his beignet and brushed off the powdered sugar from his shirt before taking a sip of coffee. As he finished his coffee, he contemplated the information in front of him. The same questions kept plaguing him. Who did this and why? When would the killer strike again? Ledet's gut told him this killer would. This case was big, and it was going to get bigger. They needed to nail this guy before he struck again.

Although they tried to keep the grisly details of any murders from the public, someone leaked the cause of death to a local reporter. The story had been sensationalized to the point of exhaustion. Many of the "facts" being reported were not even being verified. The masses didn't care about that. The only "fact" that the public could wrap their heads and their hearts around was that a young college girl's life was cut short by a monster. At least the removal of the eyes and tongue had not been released to the public.

Now, rumors circulated about the officers and detectives of the New Orleans Police Department. The rumors speculated that this department and its staff were no longer capable of performing the duties required and could not keep the citizens of this city safe. It did not matter to rumor mongers that the officers and detectives were well trained in investigative procedures.

Detective Ledet put his fingers on his forehead and massaged his temples. His head was killing him. He had stared at these files for too long. Although he had every page memorized now, he still kept looking over them, hoping he had missed something.

He despised being at the mercy of some whack job. His stomach turned with the knowledge that they must wait for him to kill again.

Chapter 6

Grace woke up and found herself bathed in darkness. Light emerged from the far off distance, but it was faint. It steadily moved closer and became brighter.

Grace felt the sensation of flying, as if she was being transported. She became aware of the sound of water flowing freely until it crashed along the bank. A gentle breeze blew through the trees along the bank. It lifted her hair and caressed her skin. Suddenly she was freezing cold. Then her world went dark once more. She was left shivering in the dark. Her throat hurt, and it was hard to breathe.

"Please, don't hurt me anymore." She cried out in her mind, "You don't have to do this."

There was no fight left in her. She had no spirit or faith left in her soul. She was empty.

She felt herself being lifted into the air once more. The sudden movement caused an excruciating biting pain throughout her body, and she tried to scream. There was no voice to carry out the scream.

Thrown into the water backward, she felt the rocks on the bottom of the bayou floor as they cut into her back. An explosion went off inside of her head. Fireworks burst before her eyes and then there was nothing but darkness once more. Her mouth was forced open, and instantly white hot pain filled her body. The coppery metallic taste of blood filled the back of her throat. It was so hard to breath now. With every gasp of breath, she drew in fire.

Bony fingers tangled themselves in her hair and yanked. Cold water gently swayed across her body. Her eye sockets felt like red hot embers had replaced her eyeballs.

She looked up and saw the shadow of a man. She saw the lunacy in his eyes. Even in the water, she felt the feverish heat radiating from him. His eyes were black, soulless orbs.

The man yelled into the night, "You made me do this. You made me who I am. You were an evil bitch!" He slashed at the night air with his knife. He was shouting, muttering, chanting and enraged. The air was charged with his hatred. His muscles bulged, testing the very limits of his shirt.

If only she could get out of this murky water, she wouldn't be alone. No one would find her here. She would die all alone. She wanted to go home, but home was far away. Home was a distant memory.

She was exhausted. Maybe, if she laid here a short while, she would gather her strength. Little did she know her body was already lifeless. Her blood ebbed out of her body and mixed with the murky water of the bayou.

Grace walked over to the water's edge and looked down. The woman lay in the bayou amongst the branches and debris. As Grace stared at the body, the woman suddenly opened her eyelids stared at her with nothing more than hollow eye sockets. Grace bit back a scream. Sadness, pain, and despair surrounded this woman.

Her flesh was already graying, tinged white. Her lips were blue. As she continued to stare at Grace, her mouth formed a silent "O" as she lifted her right arm to point towards the road. She tried to speak, but couldn't form the words.

Chapter 7

Eva Welsh stepped off the plane in New Orleans, Louisiana and the damp, humid air greeted her. Her other two friends weren't leaving until tomorrow, but Eva wanted a day to herself. She hoped to let her hair down and get totally crazy for once in New Orleans, a city that was reputed for foolishness during Mardi Gras.

Tonight, she planned on hitting some of the local bars and maybe finding someone to bring back to her hotel room. When her friends got there the next day, they would go bar hopping and catch a few parades.

Since she had been smart and only packed a carry-on bag, Eva was able to hail a cab to take her to the hotel right away. She didn't want to delay her partying tonight. On her way to the hotel, she called her parents to let them know that she'd made it to New Orleans and would talk to them later.

As she watched the scenery pass her by, she noticed the way the taxi driver looked at her. Something about him gave her the creeps. By the time she realized she might have chosen the wrong cab, it was too late. He just looked at her with a sinister smile and continued driving.

She tried to free herself from the car, but discovered that the doors didn't open from the inside. She banged on the windows hoping to get someone's attention, but they were going too fast down the interstate now for anyone to notice. She waited in horror for whatever this man had planned for her. Fear gripped her as horrid images ran through her mind. She prayed that she saw her family once again.

As he pulled off the main road onto a dirt road that brought them deeper into the swamp, she backed far away from the door. She planned on kicking him as hard as she could, hoping to escape when he opened the door.

As she waited for him to open the door, her heart was beating so hard she swore it would beat right out of her chest. As soon as he yanked the door open, Eva kicked with all her might. He just laughed at her futile attempts. As he dragged her from the car, she reached for something to grab.

She begged him, "Please let me go. I promise I won't say a thing. I just want to go home."

He threw her over his shoulders as if she weighed nothing. As the paralyzing terror took over, she knew that her time on this earth had come to an end. She turned her head and stared directly at the man who carried her off to her doom. If nothing else, she wanted his face to be burned into her soul for eternity, so that she could come back to haunt him.

When he dropped her on the ground unmercifully, she saw the flash of the blade. She felt the searing pain as it tore into her tender flesh just as she drifted into unconsciousness.

***

He watched her eyes as life left her body. Unable to resist, he bent down and kissed her. He breathed in her sweet perfume as it mixed with the coppery scent of her blood. It was an intoxicating smell.

As he prepared the body, the voices in his head started talking. The only way to silence them was to remove her eyes and tongue. Once his ritual was complete, he carried her off to her watery grave.

***

Everett Picou couldn't wait to drop his line in the water. He had been dreaming of this fishing trip all week. He told his wife, Kara, nothing was stopping him from getting up at the crack of dawn and going out today. Come rain or shine he was getting out on the water and fishing.

As he went to set his boat in the bayou, an object floating in the water caught his attention. He pulled out his flashlight and shined it over at the object to make sure that he wasn't getting ready to walk up on an alligator. He felt himself grow weak from the sight in front of him. As he made the sign of the cross over the body, he called 911 to let the dispatcher know a dead body was in the bayou. There was no doubt this poor woman was dead. The poor girl's eyes were missing.

***

Detective Ledet couldn't believe that he was driving out to another crime scene. He looked over at his partner and noticed that his face showed no emotion. Could it be his lack of emotion was due to lack of compassion? Both of them had thrown their whole life into their work, even to the point of not making time for anything else. Ledet tried his best to keep himself detached from a very emotional situation, at least long enough to do his job.

Ledet gripped the steering wheel tighter as he drove to the crime scene. As they left the city, they fought the heavy rush hour traffic on the Westbank Expressway. It was slow moving to Westwego; generally he enjoyed watching as the scenery changed from city to bayou, but that was not the case this morning.

His gut clenched in dread as he once again prepared to face a lifeless soul violently taken from this earth. He searched for the pack of cigarettes he'd hidden in his center console. He picked a hell of a time to quit smoking. The gum worked well, but the stress of this case ate away at him. It took a soulless bastard to kill another human being maliciously.

After years of working in homicide, he saw how twisted the human mind could be. It was as if senseless violence plagued this city he came to love.   Just when they solved one case, another evil infiltrated this city.

With the discovery of the latest victim's body, he was convinced this killer had no intentions of stopping. He would even bet his next paycheck that this guy was poised and ready to strike again.

By the time Detectives Ledet and Bryant made it to the crime scene, the sun was rising. Police cars lined the road as uniformed officers combed the area for clues.

Ledet walked stoically over to the bayou, passing crime scene technicians along the way. "Have you found anything yet?" The cop just shook his head and continued working.

He saw the body lying near a clump of cypress stumps. At least the media hadn't caught wind of the latest murder. Hopefully, by the time they found out, the scene would be processed, and the body removed.

Even before looking at the body, they knew what they would see. The killer's calling card was all too familiar to them now. When he saw the missing eyes, he started barking orders. "I want this entire area combed for clues. For once, I hope this guy left us something to go on."

Ledet and Bryant carefully walked around the body, being mindful of where they stepped. They looked at the body from every possible angle. Bryant sighed, "These women have the same hair color and body style. Something tells me that the victim had brown eyes as well."

Ledet just nodded his head as he continued to examine the body. He hoped they found some evidence here that gave them a clue to who this killer was. So far, nothing had been found on the bodies or crime scenes to identify a suspect. He looked over the crime scene and started the meticulous, precise task of assessing the scene. One of the crime scene techs hollered, "We have tire treads not far from where the body was discovered. They are further down the road than our boater was so they might belong to the killer."

Ledet and Bryant followed the young tech to see what they'd found. When they arrived, another tech was busy preparing to cast the tire tracks, "We also found footprints leading away from where the car was parked. We can't guarantee that these belong to the killer, but if you follow the path, it leads right to the bayou."

Ledet looked in the direction of the footprints. Could it be that they were finally catching a break? "The body has been here a couple of days though. The tire tracks and footprints from the killer should have washed away by now."

The tech shook his head, "It hasn't rained in a few days, and the ground is still moist from the last rain. Nature helped preserve the rest for us."

Bryant exclaimed, "I'll be damned. Cast everything in case this was our killer. If nothing else, maybe we can find out what kind of tires are on the vehicle."

Dr. Ortego arrived as they were making it back to where the body was located. He looked over the body and let out a sigh, "It's a damn shame. She looks so young." He asked, "Did you find any identification on her?"

Ledet shook his head, "There was nothing at the crime scene. If there was anything in her pockets, I doubt we will be able to use it. The water probably disintegrated whatever was in there."

"I'll take extra care when we get the body back to the morgue. If I find something, I will let you know."

Ledet turned to one of the crime scene techs, "Let's run her prints in case she is in the system."

After Dr. Ortego had finished examining the body, he stated, "I don't see any scars, marks or tattoos that will make it easier to identify the body. Maybe after a more thorough exam, I will find something."

"My guess is he parked close enough to carry her to the water. I don't see any indication that she was killed anywhere near this vicinity."

It took several hours for the forensics team to finish combing the area; unfortunately, they didn't find much to go on. Their only clue could be the tire tracks found, and Ledet wasn't putting too much hope into that either. Whoever did this didn't leave any personal belongings on her. The killer didn't want her to be identified. Ledet hoped that she was reported missing, and it wouldn't be a long exhaustive search to find out who this poor woman was.

Someone out there had to be missing this poor young woman. As much as he hated the daunting task of notifying the family, someone had to do it. Dread and sorrow washed over him as he thought about her family and what they were about to be put through.

By the time Ledet and Bryant walked into the police station, they looked as if they hadn't slept in twenty-four hours. Neither man took the time to shower this morning, so they desperately needed to freshen up. But that luxury had to wait a little while longer. There was still a lot to do before either man could go home.

Chapter 8

A chill ran down Hutch's spine as Mike zipped up the back of her ball gown. She was ecstatic to attend tonight's Mardi Gras Ball even if he wasn't. She had never attended one and was anxious to find out why these balls were so popular. Tonight's ball included the Who's Who in New Orleans.

When she turned around to thank Mike, her breath caught, "You are a very handsome man in that tuxedo. We should find other places for you to wear it."

He tugged once more on the bow tie, "That's okay. I can't wait to get back home and get out of this monkey suit."

She reached up and kissed him, "Mmmm, I like the idea of undressing you, but first, I want to go see why everyone goes crazy for these balls."

Mike rolled his eyes as they left the house. She knew that he did not want to rub elbows with the rich and famous of New Orleans. He couldn't understand why they were invited. The invitation was sent anonymously, as most were. They didn't even hang out with anyone who went to this type of function, so neither of them had any idea who'd sent them an invitation.

As soon as they walked into the ballroom of Chateau Orleans, Hutch's breath was taken away. She felt underdressed in her body hugging gown as she looked at the other women here. It was as if she'd stepped back in time. The women here wore voluminous satin gowns with their hair piled high on top of their heads. Their feathered masks were ornately decorated and probably cost more than her dress alone. Hutch readjusted her mask once more as Mike escorted her inside the fancy room. All around the room were exquisite Mardi Gras decorations. Wherever you looked, you caught a glimpse of purple, gold or green. The whole setting in front of her portrayed a vibrant picture of New Orleans' decadent past.

Mike bent down and whispered in her ear, "Do you feel as out of place as I do?"

Hutch nodded her head in agreement, "Just a little. I feel underdressed in what I am wearing."

He gave her a quick squeeze, "You are the most beautiful woman here. Now, how about I get us a drink?"

"That would be lovely."

As Mike went to the bar, Hutch looked around the room. She noticed a man heading her way. The way he moved rang familiar to her, but she couldn't place it. Unlike the others here, he wore a simple white mask that covered his whole face. She wondered if he was responsible for their invitation and was coming to make the proper introductions.

He spoke in a dark, raspy voice, "Detective Hutcherson, I am so glad that you made it."

"You have me at a disadvantage. You know who I am, but I don't know who you are."

He let out a soft chuckle and took her hand in his, "Oh, you soon will know who I am."

As soon as he touched her, she felt an electrical charge go through her body. The room went dark and her world silent. She felt a hand on her neck, tilting it up. She felt the cold blade against her skin, the tip puncturing her tender flesh. Horrifying images flashed through her mind. She saw bodies being disposed of in the warm, murky waters of the bayou.

Suddenly, her world went black. She had difficulty breathing. She forcefully pulled her hand from his as she grasped her neck. He watched as she struggled for air, making no move to help. He leaned in close, "I just had to know." With that short explanation, he disappeared.

Frigid ice water replaced the blood in her veins as she sank into the murky abyss of the bayou water. She was powerless. She crumpled to the floor as she struggled to take a breath. She barely felt Mike's arms wrap around her.

He waved his hands for everyone to back away, "Let's give her some air, please."

Mike worried about Hutch until he saw her eyelids flutter. "Are you all right?"

She sputtered, "Where did he go?"

Mike looked at her, puzzled, "Who?"

"A man was here a moment ago. He wore a white mask."

"Honey, I never saw a man."

Hutch shook her head in disbelief, "No, there was a man here I am sure of it. When he shook my hand, I saw what was in his mind." Hutch knew that he wasn't a figment of her imagination or even a ghost. He was a real, flesh and blood man - a very evil man at that.

Mike sensed there was more to it than what she said, "What exactly did you see?"

"Murder, I saw murder. I felt the thrill he got when he killed a person. The victim's ghost reached out to me asking for help."

Unable to enjoy the party, they went back home. Hutch couldn't explain what had happened to her tonight. It was something new that she'd experienced. Pictures flashed through her mind once more. Scenes of mutilated faces and blood ran through her mind.

She recalled the tall stranger. How did he know who she was and what she could do? Very few people knew about her "gifts" and even then, she didn't know with a simple touched she could see into their minds. He had been very bold. He wanted to see if she picked up any vibes from him.

A shiver ran through her body as the realization hit her that he'd touched her with the very hand he'd used to kill. She felt the woman's fear and his excitement.

Sleep eluded Hutch. She tossed and turned; her attempts to banish the image of the woman being murdered were futile. She couldn't erase the horror from her mind.

Giving up on sleep, she threw back the covers and hoped that a run would help to clear her mind. As she walked out the door for her run, a cool breeze gently lifted her hair. She also caught a heavy floral scent in the breeze. Even as she ran, she thought about the gruesome vision.

She considered this new chapter in her life. Was last night's experience another progression of her "gift"? How did this killer know to seek her out?

As she neared her apartment, she heard footsteps fast approaching. Fear gripped her as she quickened her pace. She almost jumped out of her skin when the runner passed her. She had to laugh at her sudden foolishness. As she let herself back into the apartment, the smell of coffee greeted her.

Chapter 9

Gabrielle heard her doorbell ring and couldn't contain her excitement. She had been excited about tonight's date and barely kept her mind on her work. She knew little about him, but he seemed to be a nice guy. It seemed as if she dated nothing but losers, but perhaps meeting him at church was a sign. She let out a gasp when she opened the door. He had a large bouquet of pink variegated roses with Asiatic lilies and the lightest pink tea roses. She brought the bouquet to her nose and breathed in the fragrant scent of the beautiful blooms.

"These are lovely."

"When I saw these, I thought of you instantly. Their beauty cannot begin to compare to your beauty. You are simply ravishing tonight."

"Well, thank you."

He asked her, "Are you ready to go out to supper?"

"I am famished."

He escorted her outside and opened the car door for her. His car impressed Gabrielle. She pictured someone like him driving a two door sports car, but the Cadillac DTS fit him. It was her favorite color, red. "I'm impressed; I took you for more of a sports car person."

He grinned, "I am a car fanatic, but I also need a car that I fit into. I don't fit into most sports cars. When I saw this car on the car lot, I knew I had to have one. It has a V8 and handles the road superbly.”

“So where are we going for supper?”

“I made reservations at Giovanni’s.”

Gabrielle stated, “That is one of my favorite restaurants. Italian food is my favorite.”

“I’ve never been to Giovanni’s.”

“You won’t be disappointed. I love their lasagna, but the pizza is good too.”

The ride to the restaurant was quiet. Both were unsure of what to say. Gabrielle rested her head back against the headrest and let the luxury of the car relax her. She took in the beautiful night. The moonlight danced across the languid waves. She could get lost in the slow, steady waves as they caressed the bank.

Once seated at the restaurant, he ordered a bottle of the house Chianti and the calamari for an appetizer.

Over wine and appetizers, Gabrielle talked about her childhood. She asked about his childhood, “I’ve done nothing but talk about me. What about you? What was it like growing up here?”

“Mine was nothing special. I was a loner. I want to hear about you tonight.”

The night passed quickly, and before they knew it, the waiter was telling them that they would be closing soon.

Gabrielle gasped in surprise, "I didn't realize we talked this long."

As he escorted her back to his car, he said, "It has been such a pleasant evening. I hate to see it come to an end."

"Same here, I can't think of the last time I had such a pleasant date. I don't get out that much."

He asked, "Would you like to get together again?"

"I'd like that very much."

Looking into her eyes, "Work has been crazy lately, but I want to take you out to supper again. I can't remember the last time I had such a pleasant evening talking to another individual. I have to admit that I almost lost the nerve to speak to you that morning at church."

Gabrielle reached over and touched his face, "I am so glad that you did."

When they arrived back at her house, he went around and opened the car door for her. He took her hand in his and escorted her to the front door. He placed a finger under her chin and tilted her face up, bent down and kissed her gently, "Good night cher."

She was speechless. His kiss, although gentle, shook her to the core. She looked into his eyes and anxiously waited for him to kiss her again. Instead, he took the keys from her and unlocked her door, "Thank you for the company tonight. We will have to do this again."

Gabrielle watched as he drove away, wondering if she would hear from him again. She hoped so. Her mind was still reeling from the goodnight kiss.

***

On the way home, his mother's nagging couldn't be ignored any longer. She started plaguing him as soon as he kissed Gabrielle. "She is a whore. All girls want is sex. Is that what you want too, you filthy little boy? Sex gives you nothing but headaches. Look what happened when I had sex, I got pregnant with the likes of you."

He looked at the clock. It was still relatively early for New Orleans; there should be someone downtown. He wished he had a different vehicle. He needed to be careful as this car was noticeable. The taxi cab blended into the city, but not this car.

It had been the perfect dinner with Gabrielle until his mother showed up. He wanted his mother to allow him to pursue a relationship with Gabrielle. She may be the one for him.

It was the perfect night for hunting. He looked up to the sky; the moon was a bright orb hanging in the black sky and the stars twinkled in the background. An urgency to silence his mother pushed him forward. As he turned down his favorite alleyway, he saw a figure rummaging through a dumpster. This may be just the person he needed.

***

Stephanie Young had big dreams while in high school, but soon afterwards, those dreams became lost to the drugs she desperately needed to calm the storm in her body. She once dreamed of becoming a model or maybe even an actress. Her parents allowed her to attend drama clubs and she tried out for any production that came to New Orleans. She had been easily misled, and that was when her drug problem started. The money rolled in, and someone was always near the set with drugs for sale. At first, she dabbled in drugs to take the edge off of her nerves. Soon, the drugs took control of her body, and she lost parts in movies. No one in the industry wanted a strung out teenager working on their set. Her shame kept her from telling her parents about her addiction. She started working in one of the strip clubs here in New Orleans; there was an abundance of them here. She quickly realized that the strip clubs paid better than working on the set.

Her parents attempted to get her into rehabilitation, but after several attempts, they finally gave up on her and left her to her own devices. Now at twenty-two years old, she was homeless and dug through dumpsters searching for booze or food. Although booze was always better.

The stillness of the night was eerily peaceful, a peacefulness that would soon be taken over by pure evil. Stephanie couldn't remember the last time downtown had been this quiet. Tonight was busy, and she didn't take the time to eat. Her plans for now were to rummage through this dumpster hoping to find something to eat or drink and then crashing until daybreak.

The hairs on the back of Stephanie's neck rose. She felt a predator's eyes upon her, watching her every move. *Stop it!*

She stopped and listened. She barely made out the sound, but it seemed as if footsteps were coming up from behind. She felt the cold steel of the blade on her neck, and before she could react, she was dead. Her body fell effortlessly to the ground.

***

A moan from his victims cried out through the alley as another joined their flock. As he picked up the body, he realized the woman was lighter than any of the others he had killed. Acting quickly, he removed her eyes and tongue. Then he tucked her behind the dumpster. He hoped this woman's death silenced his mother and the others for a while. Their voices demanded more lately. Even in death they were no longer afraid of him. Could it be they had an ally in Detective Hutcherson? He would show them that he was not someone who should be messed with.

Chapter 10

Hutch thought about supper at Beazell's On The Bayou all day today. This particular restaurant was her and Mike's favorite place to eat ever since they started dating. She could taste the barbecue shrimp appetizer and their famous Bloody Mary already.

The drive to the restaurant was breathtaking with the glimmer of raindrops clinging to the trees, reluctant to fall into the puddles below. A rainbow gracefully arched across the sky.

Beazell's On The Bayou had hit its stride here in New Orleans with food and service far superior to other restaurants here. The food here was transcendent. The chef delivered delicious flavors and artistically composed plates from a menu that changed daily with everything being fresh. Dinner had an energy that Grace loved. She wasn't sure if it was the happy buzz of diners or the knockout view of the bayou.

As they made their way through the crowded restaurant that buzzed with lively conversation and laughter to their table, Hutch looked around at the various decors. The hominess of the restaurant was one reason it had become so popular. The food was not only outstanding, but the atmosphere was reminiscent of several hunting camps here in South Louisiana. Whoever decorated the restaurant kept it authentic to the area. They even took the time and care to bring the outdoors inside. As you looked over the bayou, it felt as if you were part of the breathtaking scenery.

As the waiter handed them their menus, Hutch looked over at Mike and smiled. Damn, this man made her heart stop. The clothes he wore tonight emphasized his broad shoulders, trim waist, lean hips and powerful thighs. The women of New Orleans had to be upset with her for taking him off the market.

He reached across the small intimate table to take her hand in his. She felt the heat emanating from his body. When she caught a whiff of his cologne, her pulse quickened. A ravenous hunger coursed through her. They might have to take the dessert home tonight if he kept looking at her that way. Every pore in her body tingled, thirsty for his touch.

A young woman appeared before them with a pad and pen in hand, "Hi, I'm Emily. Would y'all like something from the bar?"

Mike looked up at her, "I would like a beer."

Hutch told her, "I have been dying for one of your famous Bloody Marys."

The waitress asked, "Would you like an appetizer to go with your drinks?"

Mike nodded his head, "An order of the Beazell's Barbecue Shrimp, please."

"Very good, sir. Have you decided what you want for dinner or do you need a few more minutes?"

Mike perused the menu one more time, "I would like the Crawfish Acadian, but can I please have the catfish blackened in your seasoning instead of fried?"

"Yes sir, you sure can. And you miss?"

Hutch handed her the menu, already knowing what she wanted. "I would like a bowl of your seafood gumbo, the house potato salad and some of your homemade French bread, please."

"That's an excellent choice. I had a sample of the gumbo earlier, and it is excellent tonight."

Hutch just looked up at the waitress and smiled. She knew what she wanted before they even arrived. Even with so many excellent items to choose from, she'd craved gumbo lately.

The waitress collected their menus, "I'll be right back with your drinks."

As Hutch broke open one of the fresh rolls placed on the table, a thin mist snaked through Hutch's vision. Hutch squeezed her eyes shut, hoping to ward off this vision. This wasn't the place she wanted to see a serial killer's victims.

Instead of dissipating though, the mist moved over her; it grew thicker and darker. It slowly consumed the light around her. The noise from the restaurant buzzing around her fell silent, and even the warmth of the air turned bitterly cold. There was nothing left for her to see except the thick gray fog and the cold emptiness it created. Through the fog, a light appeared in the center. The light became larger as it took shape. Standing in the middle of the mist was Rayne Simoneaud, and she wasn't alone. All around her were the ghosts of the serial killer's victims.

It made more sense to Hutch now. Rayne found these victims and sent them to her for help. The vision before her changed as it played out like an old silent movie. A man dressed in black waited in a dark alley. Hands reached out and grabbed the unsuspecting woman. Before she had a chance to scream, the knife sliced her throat from ear to ear. He dragged the body over to a waiting car.

Hutch watched in horror as he dropped the body in the trunk. As he closed the trunk, she caught a glimpse of a sign on top of the car. The killer was driving a taxi. This was how he found his victims. Most of these poor women got in the car willingly with him, trusting him to take them where they needed to go. It may be the first break they had in the case. The biggest problem would be finding this particular taxi in the city.

The images faded, and the mist whirled away, as if blown away by a gentle breeze. Hutch looked up to see Mike holding her hand. She forgot where she was. She pressed her fingers to her aching temples in an attempt to find some relief from the beginnings of this migraine headache. This was her first vision out in the open. It left her shivering and weak. She tried to focus on her surroundings.

Hutch glanced around as the conversation hummed at the nearby tables. No one stared at her or even noticed she had zoned out, except for Mike.   He asked, "Are you okay?"

She nodded her head, "Yes. I know now how he finds his victims. He drives a taxi."

"Did he kill another?"

She shook her head, "I don't think so. Rayne Simoneaud was in the dream. She learned something from one victim and chose this moment to show me."

Mike asked, "Do you want to leave?"

While she wanted to leave, she was also terrified her legs wouldn't hold her up, "No, let's stay and enjoy our meal."

With trembling hands, she picked up her Bloody Mary and took a sip of the zingy concoction. The drink seemed to help, and she continued to sip it. She felt stronger with each sip; although, it could be the alcohol helping her.

As the dizziness faded away, the waitress arrived with their appetizers. The smell of the food helped lighten her mood. She watched as the steam floated upwards and dissipated. This may be just what she needed to comfort her. Unable to resist the tempting smells, she dove into the barbecue shrimp.

The rich, buttery sauce coated her tongue as the spices came alive in her mouth. The shrimp were plump and tender. She moaned in ecstasy as she ate.

Mike laughed as she enjoyed her food. The sound of his laughter made her insides nice and warm.

They talked throughout dinner. As they walked back to the car, he placed his hand on the small of her back. Just this simple gesture meant so much to her. It made her feel special and protected.

Chapter 11

On his way home, he stopped at an out of the way bar and grill for a drink and a quick bite to eat. For a weekday, the joint was busy. He sat at a table in the back, secluded by darkness.

The bartender hollered over to him, "What can I get for you mon ami?"

"Double bacon cheeseburger, fries and a pale ale."

"Coming right up."

As he waited for his food, he surveyed the area. It looked as if he'd chosen the right place. He didn't see any familiar faces here. He could eat in peace and quiet before leaving.

The waitress placed the greasy, yet aromatic, bacon cheeseburger and even greasier fries in front of him and an ice cold mug of pale ale. As he went to bite into the juicy goodness of the burger, a voluptuous brown haired goddess sat down at the table with him. She picked up a fry, seductively dipped it in the ketchup he'd just poured and placed it in her mouth, gently sucking off some of the ketchup before eating the fry.

Her hair was thick and wavy. Her cleavage spilled out of her tight, way too short dress. He felt his groin stir. She looked at him with her big brown doe eyes, "I haven't seen you in here before honey."

He bit deep into the cheeseburger, savoring the well-seasoned morsel, "First time."

He took another enthusiastic bite of his burger while looking her up and down. She asked, "You have plans for tonight."

He took a swig of beer before replying, "Nope. Just came in for a bite to eat before heading home."

She let out a flirtatious laugh, "Got a wife waiting at home for you?"

As he bit into his burger once more, he felt a change in the atmosphere. Something dark and ominous seemed to have moved into the bar. Shadows rippled out of the walls like a pebble being dropped into a puddle of water. They had no distinct form, but he knew what they were. He stopped eating and watched, waiting for the shapes to take form. It had to be a trick of light. They could not have found him here.

The woman didn't seem to notice his quietness. She linked her hands around his massive forearm and whispered in his ear, "Why don't we get out of here?"

He tried to focus on the woman, but his eyes kept wandering over to the shadows as they took form. It was the ghosts of those who haunted his every movement; although, they were keeping to the shadows. As hard as he tried to bring his focus back to the voluptuous brunette, his gaze traveled back to the shadows.

Looking over her shoulder to see what he kept staring at, she asked, "What is back there? Who could possibly be more interesting than me?"

He looked into her eyes and saw his mother once more, "Nothing. I'm sorry. You said something about getting out of here?"

She smiled at him as the tip of her tongue slipped out of her mouth and moved back and forth along her lips. "You up for the ride of your life honey?"

Suddenly the shadows moved in closer to him. He stood up abruptly, knocking his chair to the ground in his haste to get the hell out of there. He grasped her arm, pulled her through the crowd of people on the dance floor and out the door.

The need to kill was too strong to go far. He pulled her into the alley. She started to protest, "Aren't we going to go back to your place honey?"

"Too far away."

"Oh baby, you are anxious aren't you."

He gave her a wicked smile, "You have no idea."

As soon as he was sure they were deep enough, he pushed her against the brick wall. In one swift movement, he had the knife out and slit her throat wide open. She fell ungracefully to the ground. Blood spewed from the massive gap. He wiped the knife and his hands on the back of her dress. Never even bothering to look at the body, he calmly walked back to his car. He kept to the shadows in case he had any blood on him.

Chapter 12

Horris Washington had worked for this current waste management company for about six months now. He preferred doing his routes in the early morning hours. The roads were nice and quiet, as if he was in his own little world. As he headed down the tight alleyway, he saw something near the rear of the dumpster. It looked as if someone had passed out in the alley. Several drivers talked about finding the homeless sleeping near dumpsters. They were instructed to wake the person up so they could move out of the way. The company didn't want a lawsuit being filed against them just because a drunk or druggy was too out of it to move the hell out of the way.

He took his flashlight out of the truck and hollered, "Hey, you need to wake up and move now, okay?" When the figure didn't move, he moved closer and shined the flashlight where the face should be. Horris would never erase the image from his mind. This was his first body to stumble upon and hopefully his last. He hurried back to his truck, pulled out his revolver, made sure the doors were locked tight and called 911.

***

Detective Ledet spotted the flashing lights from the patrol cars parked at the entrance of the alleyway. An officer came up to Ledet as he stepped out of his vehicle. "Sir, we are still waiting for the coroner."

Ledet watched as Dr. Ortego got out of his van, "Doc, sorry to drag you out at his hour."

They walked over to the body. The smell of death still bothered Ledet. Dr. Ortego pointed out some details, "It's your guy. It was risky killing her here. Even at night, there is a lot of foot traffic in this area."

"How long has she been dead, doc?"

"Rigor hasn't set in. I'd say death was in the last couple of hours."

Ledet tried to keep his emotions under control when working a case, but this time he couldn't help but feel for this poor girl. This killer treated her no better than a piece of trash.

"I don't see any defensive wounds. It looks as if he killed her quickly."

Ledet let out a string of curse words as the scene was finished being processed.

Chapter 13

Hutch felt herself falling in the dream. She felt as if she was falling into a deep, dark abyss. She tried to wake up, but her mind and body refused to cooperate. It was as if something was preventing her from waking up.

In her dream, she heard the sound of running water somewhere in the distance. She felt the cool night air on her skin and the pelting rain as it hit her body. Even in her dream, she was aware of the sights and sounds of the night. Her thoughts began to race. Was this a dream or another vision?

As Hutch stood in the darkness of the night, she felt disoriented and frightened. She looked around to find herself in the middle of nowhere; yet, there was something strangely familiar about this place.

Suddenly, it felt as if something or someone was pushing her backwards. When she looked down, she was at the edge of the bayou and about to fall in. As she peered into the water, she could make out a shape. Then a figure emerged from the watery grave. The woman had long brown hair, which was wet and matted against her face. Her drenched clothes were torn and tattered. Where the woman's eyes had once been were now empty orbs.

The young woman pointed to the road. In the distance, Hutch saw a vehicle leaving. As she watched, the taillights drove off. Hutch believed it was a car. She noticed something on top of the car. It was too dark to get a clear picture, but it appeared to be a sign.

The car suddenly stopped and backed up. It was as if the driver sensed she was out here. Hutch tried to make out the sign on top of the vehicle as it came closer to her. In her dream, Hutch felt someone shaking her.

Mike heard Hutch breathing heavy. After what she had been through, he worried that she was having another nightmare. "Grace… Grace…… Grace!"

Hutch bolted upright in bed to find Mike looking at her. She grabbed on to him tight, needing his arms around her. "Oh Mike, the killer struck again. The girl called out to me. He just left her body in the bayou. "

"Did you notice anything that may help us find the killer?"

Hutch shook her head, "No, not really. There was a sign on top of his car, but I couldn't make it out."

"It's time we went and talked to the detectives working on this case. Maybe they will be open minded enough to listen to what you have to say."

Hutch shook her head, "I don't know Mike. I don't mind that you and Guy know the dead talk to me, but I don't want the rest of the department looking at me like I have lost my mind."

Mike wrapped his arms around Hutch, "If they want this case solved, they will listen to what you have to say."

Hutch fell into a fitful sleep, and several hours later woke up feeling as if she hadn't slept at all. After the vision, it had been a restless sleep. Her eyes were weary and grainy, as if the insides of her eyelids were sandpaper.

She woke up to find that Mike had already gotten out of bed. The room was gray and full of ominous shadows. The curtains were drawn tight, allowing little light to enter the room. Stretching, she stepped out of bed and pulled open the curtains. Bright sunlight poured into the room, removing any remaining shadows.

She heard Mike in the master bathroom and headed that way. As she brushed her teeth, she stared at her face in the mirror. She was still pale from last night's vision. Her eyes were red and puffy. Her hair was tangled as if she had been tossing and turning all night. She slipped out of her nightclothes and joined Mike in the shower.

On the drive over to the police station, Hutch worried about telling other detectives about her "gift". It may be a ridiculous fear, but a very real fear. Over the years, her gift had helped her with her job, but from her experience, people were uncomfortable with things that couldn't be explained. Most people became wary if there wasn't a logical explanation, or they couldn't laugh it off. She learned that even those who said they were open minded tended to back off if things didn't fit into whatever mold they'd created for their lives.

It didn't help that her "gift" had manifested into something different than what she grew up with. In the past, she only used her "gift" when there was a need, such as walking through a crime scene. Now, she had a hard time controlling her "gift". She could be walking along and suddenly have a vision. Was this how it would be from now on?

By the time they reached the police station, Mike had found out who was handling the case. She reluctantly followed Mike to the conference room, "Detective Ledet, I want you to meet Detective Hutcherson."

Ledet extended his hand to Hutch. She gave it a firm handshake as she eyed Mike suspiciously. Detective Ledet went on to state, "Detective Bailey filled me in on some of what you have seen. We are indeed working on a case where the victims' eyes are removed. This morning's victim was discovered in a bayou not far from New Orleans."

Hutch mournfully shook her head, "I had hoped that the visions were from a cold case murder. How many bodies have been found to date?"

"So far three bodies were found, but I believe there are more we don't know about. I must warn you, when Detective Bailey told me I thought this was ridiculous. However, he assures me that what you are witnessing is very real."

"Trust me, I wouldn't come forward with my 'gift' if I didn't think it was necessary. I don't want to be judged by my colleagues. I can't explain how it works or when a vision will appear, but it just does."

"How many do you suspect he has killed?"

"I believe two tried to contact me, but I can't be certain of that either." Hutch suspected Rayne Simoneaud sent the troubled spirits her way so she could help them move on. She needed to find out what Rayne knew about these recent murders. She also wanted to see where the body was found this morning. "Where was the body found? I may be able to pick up on the victim's last moments and find out more on this killer."

As Hutch and Mike drove to the crime scene, she tried to take her mind off of the actual murder. She watched the scenery change as they left the city to the gnarly regions of the bayou. As Mike's car slowly made its way down the dirt road leading to the bayou, Hutch found herself bouncing in the seat. She had to get a firm grip on the handle above the door frame to keep focused on the scenery in front of her. The killer came this way. She should be able to pick up some sort of vibe the killer left behind.

When they arrived at the crime scene, no one was there to bother her. Hutch concentrated on the ground as she began to survey the scene. She had to pick her way through the areas heavy with twisted growth. The air was heady with the scent of cypress and damp earth. The sun beat down on her as she walked to the bayou. The hideous scene began to play out in front of her, similar to fragments of a movie playing.

Engrossed in the scene playing out in front of her, she didn't hear Mike come up behind her. She jumped when he placed his hands on her shoulder. "I'm sorry. I should have warned you I was coming."

She let out a laugh and leaned back on him, "I completely forgot you were here. I was trying to make out what happened the night of her murder."

"Were you able to piece any of it together?"

She shook her head, "No, not really. It came in as distorted images. The other night while dreaming I could have sworn the killer had backed up when he saw me out here."

Mike held onto Hutch tighter, "Do you think he is somehow connected to you as well?"

"No, that's not it. It is hard to explain. It's as if he saw me standing out here in his rearview mirror and was surprised."

Chapter 14

Gabrielle walked in the door, kicked off her high heels and removed the confining clothes. Today had been a trying day. Normally, she enjoyed crunching numbers, but with tax season here and the deadline near, it was crazy. Nothing went right. A new client walked in the door with ten years of taxes needing to be filed. Then one client's tax returns had been returned; he'd forgotten about some extra income and failed to report it. On top of everything else going on, one of the attorneys they bill for settled a large case and needed to disperse checks for it.

To make matters worse, the new receptionist had no people skills. She dropped calls and several clients called on the back line, refusing to talk with her.

At times, Gabrielle considered changing jobs or opening her own business, but she barely made ends meet as it was. Opening her own business could financially bankrupt her. As far as a new job, there weren't many jobs out there unless she wanted to wait tables or flip burgers. For now, she was stuck working for Mr. Chaisson. At least he was a nice man who treated his employees well. She'd worked there for three years now and never had a problem with him. He always treated her fairly.

Maybe what she needed tonight was to let her hair down. It had been a while since she'd gone to the club.

Shaking her head, she should stay home tonight. She was already tired and wouldn't be able to enjoy the club. After changing into something more comfortable, she went into the kitchen to cook a quick supper. She rummaged through the fridge and grimaced at the lack of food. Letting out a sigh, she settled on a grilled cheese sandwich.

Once it was cooked, she grabbed her plate and headed to the living room. Flipping through the channels, she found a movie she hadn't seen in ages. However, no matter how hard she tried to concentrate on the movie, her mind kept going back to her date the other night. As she finished supper, the phone rang, "Hello."

"I didn't catch you at a bad time did I? I wanted to call you for the past few days, but I didn't want to scare you off either."

She responded quickly, "Oh no, I am so glad you called. I'm unwinding from a hectic day at work."

"Would you like to go out Saturday night?"

Hoping she didn't answer too hastily, she blurted out, "That would be great."

They talked for several more minutes before finalizing plans for Saturday night.

Chapter 15

The photographs of the young women stared back at Ledet from the murder board. Their faces were so young and vibrant before the killer cut their lives short. These women had been so full of life and deserved to grow old. Instead, they were cheated out of a life.

Next, his eyes traveled to the pictures of what remained of their faces. The grisly shadows of where their eyes once were stared back at him.

He wanted to avert his eyes from the hollowed out sockets that stared back at him, but he didn't. He needed to see them, needed to remember them. Anger welled up inside of him. He let the obsession of finding this killer overcome him. He wouldn't stop looking at the pictures until they were burned into his mind. He would find who did this to these beautiful women. He'd promised their families that he would catch this killer.

Bryant walked into the room, "We identified the latest victim. Her family just filed the missing person's report. She came to New Orleans for vacation and hasn't been heard from since. Her friends arrived after her and found that she hadn't checked into the hotel room. They called her parents, worried that maybe she hadn't been able to make it. We confirmed with the airport that she flew into New Orleans, and that was the last anyone has heard from her."

"Let's go to the airport and check out the security tapes."

"That'll work. It gives us some time before her parents arrive. Even though we identified the body, they still want to come down."

By the time Bryant and Ledet made it back to the police station, Eva Welsh's parents had arrived. Mrs. Welsh sat at his desk with tears threatening to spill at any moment. She dabbed the corner of her eyes. They stood up as soon as they saw the two detectives heading their way.

"Detectives, do you really believe it is her?"

Bryant took the mother's hands in his, "I am sorry for your loss. The coroner's office confirmed that it is indeed your daughter."

Mr. Welsh asked, "Do you think we can see her?"

Ledet shook his head, "You don't want to remember her like this sir. Please sir, remember her how you last saw her."

Mr. Welsh asked, "What did he do to our daughter?"

"Her face was mutilated after she died, sir."

Mrs. Welsh gasped, "Did she suffer? Was she tortured… or… worse?"

Bryant informed her, "No, ma'am, she didn't suffer, but we do ask that you keep what happened to your daughter to yourselves. We don't want to alert the media just yet. It could seriously compromise our case. Do you understand?"

They both nodded in unison, "When do you think we can take her back home?"

Ledet replied, "I'm not sure when we can release her to you, but we will try to do it as soon as possible."

Chapter 16

All Gabrielle thought about was her date tonight. The week had dragged on. She didn't think Saturday would ever get here. In case tonight went as planned, she picked up some protection from the store and put clean sheets on the bed.

She took an extra-long time getting ready. Tonight, she wanted his eyes on her and not another woman.

A shudder of anticipation ran through her as she thought about this evening. The man was hot. She could only imagine what he would be like in bed. They seemed to be perfect for each other.

Butterflies fluttered around in her stomach as she waited for him. She didn't want to appear overly anxious, but she couldn't wait for him to arrive. As nervous as she was, you would think this was their first date. She had opened the door before he had a chance to knock. He bent down and kissed her lightly on the lips. The simple kiss left her wanting more.

***

On the drive to the restaurant, Gabrielle talked non-stop. He listened intently to her every word. She talked so much that it helped drown out his mother's constant nagging in his other ear.

When they arrived at Antoine's, she noticed the line. "This place is really popular tonight. I'm not sure we will ever get a table." The line wrapped around the corner of the building.

Instead of waiting in line, he walked up to the hostess and gave her his name. The maître d' appeared not soon after, "Right this way sir. Everything is ready."

Gabrielle looked at him with genuine surprise, "You planned out this date tonight. I'm impressed."

He looked down at her and smiled, "I wanted everything perfect for you. We have a special table for tonight."

The maître d' escorted them to a private room near the kitchen that was bathed in candlelight. "Oh my," Gabrielle gasped, "you outdid yourself. It is absolutely beautiful."

He informed her, "I didn't want to share you with the other diners. I wanted a nice, cozy dinner so we can sit and talk."

"A girl can get spoiled being around you."

He smiled over at her, "I'm glad you agreed to go out with me again."

***

As they ate their dinner, Gabrielle couldn't take her eyes off of him. He looked dashing in his suit and tie. When he smiled at her, her heart melted. She was falling in love with him.

As they finished the seafood barquette au gratin, shrimp and crabmeat cooked in a lustrous velvety cream sauce and served in a fresh bread bowl, the waiter placed their entrees in front of them. They both elected to try the special of the night, fried redfish with an andouille sausage gravy. She moaned in ecstasy as her taste buds came to life with each bite. "Now, I understand the long line. The food is excellent."

He agreed, "The food is excellent, but the company is better."

***

He had wanted to take her to Beazell's On The Bayou, but couldn't risk running into someone he knew there. If someone he worked with saw him, he would never hear the end of it. He wasn't ready for anyone to know he was dating. The heckling would not stop.

"I wish I cooked like this. I can burn a pot of boiling water. What about you? Are you a master chef?"

"I can cook a few good dishes. My mother never took the time to cook. If I wanted to eat, I had to make it myself."

He saw the sympathy in her eyes and ridiculed himself for letting it slip about his mother. "That is the first time you mentioned your childhood."

"I'm not comfortable talking about it. It was pretty bad; besides, I would rather listen to you talk."

"I tend to talk non-stop, so don't give me free reign. As an only child, I never had anyone else to talk to besides my parents. My dad used to ask me if I ever shut up."

He laughed at the comment, "I can't imagine why he didn't want to listen to you talk."

"I always had a vivid imagination and dreamed different imaginary friends to play with."

As he listened to her talk, he noticed similarities in their childhoods. It didn't sound like she had many friends either. Still, he wasn't ready to divulge too much information about himself.

He didn't even realize the time until the lights went off in the dining room. He looked at her, "It's after two o'clock in the morning. Something tells me they are ready to close up though. I didn't realize how long we have been talking. I should take you home so that you can get some rest."

When they arrived at her house, he escorted her to her front door and kissed her lightly on the lips, "Goodnight Gabrielle. Sleep tight cher."

"Goodnight."

***

Gabrielle's heart sank as he drove off. She'd lost her nerve and didn't ask him in for a nightcap. Now, she regretted it. She would be tossing and turning all night, thinking of him. Worse, the club was already in full swing, and there wouldn't be too many partners left to pair up with. Letting out a sigh, she may as well try to get some sleep.

As she tossed and turned in bed, she wondered if he didn't find her attractive. She thought he would make a move, but he merely kissed her goodnight at the door. At first, the fact that he was such a gentleman turned her on, but now she found it annoying. If they went out on another date, she would make sure he found her sexy.

Chapter 17

The overhead lights bathed the jazz band performing on the small stage in a hazy glow. Hutch found Mike's hand on her elbow comforting as the waiter showed them to their table. Hutch took the time to look at the servers working tonight. Everyone was dressed as if they were starring in an old gangster film.

She and Mike had followed this local jazz band these last few months; trying to take in as many of their live performances as possible. They both found this new and upcoming band enjoyable. Hutch saw them making a name for themselves and doubted it would be long before someone discovered them.

Mike ordered a pale ale made by one of the local breweries and Hutch ordered a strawberry daiquiri. She needed something to help cool the heat from the hot wings Mike ordered. The wings lived up to their name of Cajun Fire Wings, but they were so good. There was a hint of something sweet used in the sauce that made them totally addictive.

Just as they began to relax, the food and drinks arrived. Without waiting for the wings to cool off, Mike picked one up, "Hot. Hot. Hot."

Hutch let out a sexy little laugh, "You could wait for them to cool down."

"What and have you eat most of them before I do?"

She just shook her head as she picked up one of the fiery drumettes, "Mmmm, I will regret this later on, but damn, these things are so good."

As her mouth turned into a volcano, she reached for her strawberry daiquiri. Mike just laughed at her watering eyes as he threw down another naked chicken bone. Licking the thick sauce off his fingers, he stated, "You are such a wuss."

She smiled over at him, "These things are so hot, but delicious at the same time. I just can't stop myself from torturing my mouth. I don't know how you put away so many without having to drink something in between."

Mike just smiled, "It's because if I slow down you will eat them all."

"There may be some truth in that."

As the night wore on, Mike saw Hutch's mood change, "Dare I ask what's wrong? Did you have another vision?"

"No, not really. I was thinking about these women. What is my connection to them? Why do I suddenly see this killer and their murders? This never happened to me before. I read scenes before, but nothing like this. It is something entirely different."

Mike stood up from his side of the table and pulled Hutch onto the dance floor. She melted into his body as they swayed to the sound of the music. This may be just what she needed to take her mind off these visions for a while, that and a few more strawberry daiquiris.

As soon as her head hit the pillow, she found herself being transported to another place. An unnatural quiet filled her mind as if the sound had been sucked out. Suddenly, she heard a cacophony of sounds fill the air. There was a chorus of crickets serenading to the moonlight and frogs calling out for their mate. Flashes of lightning snaked across the sky, and angry clouds rolled in from the south.

Thunder boomed throughout the night sky as raindrops freed themselves from their heavy confines. Ignoring the rain, her gaze focused on the bayou. The moonlight was cloaked in a misty haze. An ephemeral glow of light hung over the murky water.

The hoot of an owl echoed in the night as she made her way past the boat dock to the water's edge. Fog rolled off the water's surface as she stopped beside a pile of branches caught along the edge of the water. Rain continued to fall, and she watched as the drops danced off the bayou. An alligator's head appeared a few feet away from her, watching her every move.

The apparition moved to where she was, surrounding her in a mist of chilly air. Hutch took in the apparition's translucent skin and lifeless hair. She stared at Hutch with nothing but hollow eye sockets. "Please help us."

As Hutch reached out to touch the young woman in front of her, the image waned. A flash of lightning lit up the sky and chased away the shadows. When Hutch looked down at the bayou once more, she saw the young woman's body entangled in the maze of branches and vines at the water's edge. Her long black hair flowed in the water like seaweed. Another flash of lightning startled fish in the gaping wound they were nibbling on. Now, she knew why she was here. Dread washed over her.   Another body would be found.

As the images flashed through her mind, she had a sense of déjà vu. The previous visions were almost identical to this one.

A noise from behind caught her attention. Was that an echo of a scream uttered in the past? Could it be the sudden hush of the bayou holding its breath while waiting to see what was about to happen?

A thread of light moved through the dense thicket of trees. She crouched behind a cypress trunk and watched as the killer made his way to his car. She kept to the shadows as she continued to follow him. Perhaps, this time, she would catch a glimpse of his face.

Before she could witness anything else, her vision was cut short. She eased herself out of the bed and took special care not to wake Mike. In the bathroom, she turned on the cold water and splashed it over her heated face. Looking at her reflection in the mirror, she winced at the image staring back at her. She looked tired, and the bags under her eyes were more pronounced today than they were yesterday.

As she curled back up in bed, she prayed she could fall back asleep. Utter exhaustion consumed her as her head hit the pillow.

Hutch heard the alarm go off but didn't have the energy to lift her head off the pillow. Mike reached over and turned the blasted thing off before heading toward the bathroom.

Instead of getting out of bed, she snuggled under the covers and hoped to get in a few more minutes of sleep. Mike looked back at the bed and watched as Hutch tossed and turned. He was concerned what affect these visions were having on her. The dreams were becoming more frequent.

***

The street he planned to hunt on was devoid of life. An occasional car passed by, but that was it. Maybe he was too far from the crowds and excitement tonight. He drove for a couple of hours, searching for the perfect one. He feared that he wouldn't be able to satisfy his hunger.

This was a terrible unfamiliarity for him. As the clock reached three o'clock in the morning, he contemplated calling it a night. He should have chosen a different place to hunt. As he drove down the street, the cobblestone glistened in the rain. The moonlight bathed the area in a demonic glow. Despair grew deep inside of him as he drove away.

The night was going all wrong. Even though a storm hadn't been predicted, the weather had turned nasty. Rain beat down on the windshield as the wipers attempted to keep up with the rhythm. Up ahead, the gray skies turned black.

A movement caught his attention. He slowed down. Maybe, just maybe, this was her. He pulled the car over and hurried to where he had seen her. Not wanting to kill her here in the rain, he used his fists to knock her out cold. Acting quickly, he threw her into the trunk and drove off into the night.

He found a secluded spot along the bayou to kill her, submerging the body in the water. He must make sure no fibers remained on her for discovery.

It was close to morning by the time he arrived home. As soon as his head hit the pillow, he fell into a deep sleep. Several hours later, he bolted upright in bed as a cold chill ran over his body. He found himself covered in sweat and wrapped in soaking wet sheets. Peering through the darkness, he found the source of what had so rudely awakened him.

He was having such a good dream too before his mother's harping pierced through his dream. She had become incessant lately. He thought locking her up at the back of the cabinet would silence her, but she just grew louder.

As he tried to tune his mother out and return to his dream, he wondered if he had let his obsession for vengeance control his life? He shook his head at just how ridiculous he was being. Killing gave him a purpose; besides, it was too late to stop now. The evil lurking inside of him wanted out. It wouldn't fade away. He knew how this could end, but couldn't stop. Besides, he wanted to play some more with Detective Hutcherson.

Chapter 18

Ledet stood near the water's edge and surveyed the scene in front of him. Cypress trees grew in abundance here, both in and out of the water. Spanish moss draped from the limbs and blew gracefully in the wind. A slow moving snake slithered through the coffee colored water of the bayou. If it weren't for the scene in front of him, this would be a tranquil place.

The humidity from last night's rain clung to him. He swatted at a mosquito as he looked down at the body. A flurry of activity took place around him. Photos were being taken, and the surrounding area was combed for clues.

He heard Dr. Ortego holler out orders as his assistants removed the body from the water. Dr. Ortego looked over the body and told Ledet, "She's been dead over twelve hours."

The gaping wound on her neck appeared more grotesque than it would have at the time of death due to the water creatures attacking the body. They were lucky that the alligators hadn't dragged her off to one of their hiding holes for the body to ripen. Just how many women had become an alligator's meal?

As he walked towards Hutch, the sound of an engine caught his attention. A boat with a two stroke engine came barreling across the bayou and caused the water to ripple. It's a good thing the body was already removed from the water.

He shook his head as he thought about what happened here. He hoped that Hutch would be able to read something from the scene that they could find useful.

Chapter 19

Kayla Landry wanted to get a quick run in before the rain hit. Instead of going home and trying to beat the storm, she headed out to her car to retrieve her gym bag. She would run along the River Walk tonight. She was close to beating her time for the last marathon, and she couldn't afford to miss one day of training.

He'd just dropped off his latest ride when he saw her running along the River Walk. Even though it was almost daybreak, someone may see him, but the voices had grown louder and louder. This may be what he needed to silence them.

He zeroed in on his prey. Reaching into the glove box, he pulled out his knife. The weight and smoothness of the blade gave him a rush. He rubbed his thumb over the hilt and stared at the eight inches of well-honed serrated steel. He sped up and pulled into an alley that he believed she would run past. If he acted fast enough, he could have her silenced before anyone even knew what happened. The exhilaration of this kill was almost more than he could handle. Excitement and an exquisite rush of adrenaline surged through him as he waited.

Like the small animals he used to hunt, he waited for his prey. As quick as lightning, his arms reached out and grabbed her as she ran past the alley. Her mind never registered what happened. He slit her throat from ear to ear before she screamed.

Not wanting to leave her body in the alley and still needing to remove her eyes, he opened the trunk. He was ever so careful to lay out the tarp before placing the body in the trunk and heading out. He knew the perfect place to leave the body, but he had to wait for nightfall. That gave him plenty of time to take her home and remove her eyes before disposing of her body.

***

As he disposed of the body, he suddenly stopped and looked around. He sensed a strong presence somewhere nearby. He could not explain his feelings, but he knew better than to doubt his intuition even if he didn't see anything. It was not the first time since he started killing that he sensed someone nearby.

He looked up at the moon suspended high in the treetops and called out, "I know you are hiding nearby. You may as well come out." He patiently waited, but no one answered.

***

The bedroom was cold as ice. Her fingertips tingled, and her feet were freezing. A shiver ran through her body. Hutch bolted upright in bed choking down a scream. She looked over at the clock to see that it was only three thirty in the morning. She softly moaned; it would be impossible for her to go back to sleep.

She wasn't sure if the killer had struck again or if a victim was once again reaching out, hoping that Hutch could help her.

She looked over to see Mike sleeping peacefully. She wished he would wake up and take her into his arms. She needed the comfort of those strong arms around her right now.

She reached out and touched his shoulder. She needed to feel his warmth. She was head over heels in love with him. She loved him more than she had ever loved any other person. She hated that she put him through the stress of these visions and dreams. He never once complained though. Without him, she feared her life would spiral into nothing more than a twisted ride of nightmares that she couldn't understand.

Ghostly images appeared before her, confirming that another woman was dead. Lately, the dead refused to be ignored. She had become some sort of traiteur to the dead. As if sensing her stress, Mike wrapped his arms tightly around her and provided her some warmth. But she was still cold to the bone.

Tears welled up inside of her. She had never experienced such a vivid vision before. She actually became part of the vision. For a moment, she felt what the victim felt. At least the malevolent vision was now broken.

Disappointment filled her soul yet again, everything she witnessed about the terrifying murder and mutilation of the body gave her no clues as to the killer's identity. There was not one shred of tangible evidence she could use to begin her search.

She needed to see his face or identify him somehow. There was more to this than just the grisly murders of these innocent young women. It was up to her to stop him.

She buried her face into Mike's bare chest. The intoxicating smell of his body helped to soothe her. Just being close to him made everything seem better.

Hutch woke up to find Mike already up. She heard the sound of running water and dozed off once more. The sound of the shower helped soothe her nerves. The hum of the electric razor woke her from the edge of sleep.

For a moment, she couldn't focus on anything with details. All around her was a distant melody of sounds. It took her a moment to focus in on her surroundings. She was in an older house, surrounded by negative energy. An uncontrollable rage built up inside of her body. Her blood began to boil. Her head throbbed as her heart pounded in her chest. Monstrous thoughts took over her mind, kill, destroy and finally silence. Before she could move further into the house, an excruciating pain tore through her body. Her vision faded. She thought she heard footsteps walking away from her.

Opening her eyes, she found herself once more in her bedroom. Whatever just happened was something she had never experienced before. She had been inside the killer's house, but it was as if an unknown force kept her from moving or seeing anything before being forced out.

As he walked into the house, he fell to the floor. Pressure built within his head. He waited for his head to explode at any moment. The left side of his face went numb. The seizure took over as his body thrashed on the ground violently. He jittered as spittle dripped from the corner of his mouth.

As soon as one seizure subsided, another seizure wracked his body. After the aftershock of the seizures had subsided, his body continued to shake. After several seconds, he continued to stare at the ceiling as he relished the coolness of the floor against his back. If he sat up, the pain would take over again.

He was sluggish and drowsy, as if he had not slept in days. When the nausea took over his body, he crawled to the bathroom and prayed to the porcelain gods; afterwards, he stood up and walked to the bedroom with a clumsy, uncoordinated gait. Keeping the ghosts at bay took more out of him than letting them haunt him. She had entered the sanctuary of his house. This one was getting too close to him; he must be careful.

Chapter 20

Hutch was exhausted and frightened at the same time. Her mind was on overload and had reached its capacity. Just as she drifted back to sleep, her phone rang. She looked over at Mike, "I guess it was more than a dream." Mike didn't even reply. He started to dress. Early morning phone calls meant only one thing---someone else was murdered.

Hutch let out a sigh as they drove down the barely paved gravel road. This killer must have a good suspension system on his car because these roads played hell on you as they bounced you along. The headlights bounced along the darkened road flashing yellow beams of light along the roadway.

Mike watched the road closely, searching for the flashing lights of the other police cars working the scene. "I don't see any lights behind me so either the media are already here or they haven't found out about the murder yet."

"Let's hope for once that they don't know about the murder just yet. I'm tired of fielding their asinine questions."

Hutch looked around once more. They'd left civilization several miles back. "He has to be from here, or he researched the town well. Most of these back roads don't even show up on GPS much less maps."

Up ahead, Hutch saw the flashing lights of the police vehicles. The lights cast a fuzzy glow around the scene. Mike had grabbed a flashlight before they made their way to the crime scene. The moon hung above them, casting shadows all around. Dew clinging to the unkempt grass sparkled from the flashing strobe lights of the police cars that outlined the area. Several policemen attempted to ward off media and bystanders.

***

Detective Ledet watched as Detectives Bailey and Hutcherson made their way to the crime scene. His day had just started, and stomach acid already boiled up into his esophagus. As Hutch walked up to the crime scene, he popped an antacid into his mouth. He wanted answers now, but she had to wait for daybreak before she could get a better look at the scene.

He passed Hutch the roll of antacids, "Want one?"

Hutch shook her head and nodded to where the reporters gathered, "I see they have already heard about the latest murder."

"How did they hear about it before us? I swear they are like vultures. They smell blood and start circling."

One nosy reporter asked, "Did the killer strike again?"

Ledet turned, scowling at the pesky reporter, "Give us time to investigate would you? We just got here."

Hutch looked at him. They knew how the reporters learned about the murders, police scanners. They were responsible for these jackals making it to the crime scenes before investigators had time to get there. It would be so much easier if they kept the traffic off the police scanners, but it was next to impossible to do.

Hutch looked around the crime scene, "I see I made it here before Dr. Ortego."

"He is on his way. Something had him tied up at home."

Dr. Ortego's wife took a turn for the worse, and the chemotherapy was taking a toll on her body. All they could do for Dr. Ortego and his wife was pray. "Have you checked out the crime scene?"

"I figured I would wait for you. I was worried that if we started traipsing around the scene, it might throw you off. Bryant had to stay back at the office, something about court today. It is just you and me."

Hutch shook her head, "Well, let's see what we can find out."

As they made their way to the crime scene, the crime scene tech van arrived. As they unloaded their equipment, Ledet stated, "They won't get in our way."

As Hutch walked over to the body, she stopped. She looked up at the stars, but it's like her sudden stop had them holding their breath as well. Even the stars had waited for her next move before they twinkled once again in the night sky. Time slowly stretched forward. Goose bumps formed on her body as she brought herself to look at the body. Even though she knew the answers, she still found herself asking, "He took time with the body didn't he?"

Ledet nodded his head in agreement, "He posed this body. The victim appears to be in her early twenties."

***

Hutch took in the scene before her. The killer took his time in posing the body. Was he playing with them? He had placed one of the victim's hands over her eyes and the other over her mouth. Her clothing was torn and dirty, as if he dragged her there. Mud clung to her hair and streaks of mud blotched her face. Her face had a bluish hue; almost translucent in appearance. Even though the eyes and mouth were covered, Hutch knew what was underneath. Her delicate lips remained open in a grotesque sneer. Where once had been gorgeous brown eyes with flecks of gold were merely black voids. The air around them was alive with nervous energy. "I guess we won't know until Dr. Ortego gets here, but I'm certain he removed her eyes and tongue like the others."

Ledet agreed, "He cut her throat from ear to ear, but there is also blood on her cheeks and chin so I have to agree. I'm unsure why he covered her face the way he did."

Hutch walked around the crime scene, getting a feel for the scene. "She wasn't killed here?"

Ledet agreed, "No, there isn't enough blood at the scene. I'm not sure why he chose this area to pose her. There isn't a lot of foot traffic here. If not for the truck driver pulling over to take a leak, I doubt we would have found the body any time soon."

"Come daylight, someone would have seen her when driving by."

Mike looked around, "I'm not so sure. Even during the day, it would be difficult to see her back here. Are we sure that the truck driver isn't the doer?"

Ledet shook his head, "Crime scene techs are searching his truck, but he is pretty shaken up. I don't think he expected to find a body. From what he said, he did not notice her until zipping up his pants. Something out of the corner of his eye caught his attention. When we drove up, you could tell that the ground had been recently disturbed. Perhaps the killer had dragged her body this time instead of carrying her. This area doesn't have a lot of traffic at this hour. I suspect our truck driver hoped to take a leak and then maybe catch a little shut eye before getting back on the road."

As Mike and Ledet talked, Hutch continued to walk the scene. The image of a man appeared before her, but he was shrouded in black. As he dragged the body, he slashed the air with his knife. Hutch exclaimed, "I think he is trying to silence the victims. It is possible that the ghosts talk to him, tormenting him. That may be why he removes their tongues. As far as the eyes go, they are referred to as the windows to the soul. He could be trying to collect their souls in his own way, or he is attempting to keep them from seeing what he does. They are indeed haunting him."

Hutch turned away from the body and looked over at the horde of gawkers crowding the crime scene. Did he pose the body for the media? Was the killer counting on the body being detected early on?

She tried to read the energy here at the crime scene. If only she could get a feel for this killer, but he seemed to be able to keep himself hidden from her. By his demeanor, though, the ghosts talked to him. She tried to hone in on him as he posed the body. Suddenly, he stopped and looked back.

She swore he looked directly at her. A chill passed through her as he looked in her direction before finishing with the body. Why did he look back? Did something catch his attention last night? She instructed one of the crime scene techs, "Scan this area well, please. Let's see if someone else was here last night."

Mike came over and asked, "What do you have?"

Hutch replied, "It may be nothing, but while he posed the body, he turned and looked right where I am standing."

"This is the second time you mentioned that he seemed to look back where you were at. Do you suppose he can sense you?"

Hutch shook her head, "I don't think so. I can't explain why he looked back." Hutch moved to where the killer had stood to see if she could get a sense of what he may have heard or saw. "The ghosts of the other victims are following him. Even though he removed their eyes, they have somehow attached themselves to him. I believe that is why he slashed the air earlier. He thought he had silenced them, but it must have been unsuccessful. If only they would talk to me. Maybe one of them knows who he is or even where he lives."

Hutch tried to get their attention, but they remained focused on the killer and what he was doing at the moment. She must wait for them to reach out to her again. There had to be a way to get them to talk to her.

As Hutch finished, Dr. Ortego pulled up. As he walked over to them, she saw the depression etched on his face. He shook his head as he observed the body, "She was so damn young."

Ledet nodded his head in agreement, "We waited for you to get here before we did anything with the body."

"I am sorry it took me so long. I had to wait for my daughter to get to the house before I could leave."

Hutch put a hand on his shoulder, "We understand Dr. Ortego. It's okay."

He looked at her with an attempt of a smile on his face, "Well, let's see if this guy removed her eyes and tongue shall we?"

As he carefully moved her hands, he placed a baggie over each in case there was any trace evidence they could use. "It's your guy. The eyes and tongue were removed with surgical precision. As with the others, he slit her throat first."

***

The killer slipped into the ever growing crowd of bystanders and media gawking at the crime scene. He caught the commotion on his radio and decided to stop by to watch as they investigated his handiwork. He found this almost as thrilling as the kill itself.

From where he stood, he observed the technicians taking pictures and the coroner examining the body. He watched in fascination as the female detective walked around the crime scene instead of looking at the body. Could it be that she couldn't bring herself to look at his handiwork? A broad smile came over him at that possibility. As he watched her further though, he realized that wasn't the case. Occasionally, she looked back at the body before continuing to walk the perimeter of the crime scene. The way she carried herself wasn't like the other detectives. She was getting a feel for the actual crime scene and not worried about the body.

She moved back over to the body, staring down at the face, as if memorizing the face. At first, it upset him that the body had been found so soon. However, he may have to turn this into a little game with the detectives.

As he watched the detectives work, the voices started up once again in his head. He placed his hands over his ears in an attempt to silence them. Now was not the time to draw attention to himself.

A chill moved over Hutch. She looked up to see several of the victims standing over the body.

The killer watched in horror as the ghosts appeared over the body. This time, though, they seemed to be reaching out to the female detective. He stood frozen in place as one woman lifted her arms and pointed in his direction. Not wanting to take any chances, he decided to leave.

The killer sensed the female detective heading his way. He must find out if she could talk to ghosts. Right now, though, he must leave before she discovered his identity.

Thankfully, he parked his car further away from the crime scene than needed. He ducked into the woods to return to his car.

Once satisfied that he wasn't being followed, he pulled over to a convenience store parking lot to gather his thoughts. He must find a way to silence these ghosts, especially if they had found someone who would listen to them. He must learn more about this female detective. He wouldn't have anyone putting a stop to his killing.

***

Hutch looked up just in time to see a man walking away from the group of bystanders. She took off in his direction.

As Hutch looked around to see where the man went, Mike walked up behind her, "Our killer was here, watching the crime scene. We need to see if the crime scene techs managed to get a picture of him in the crowd."

"You believe that was the killer you followed?"

"Yes, I am positive. The ghosts of the victims appeared to me while Dr. Ortego looked over the body. They wanted to get my attention and pointed to where he stood in the crowd."

Mike walked over to the tech taking pictures, "Once you get the photos of the crowd developed, please let me know. I believe our killer was here."

The young tech nodded his head, "Yes, sir. We will get on that once we make it back to the office."

This killer was turning into her own personal nightmare, killing these poor women right under their noses. So far, they hadn't been able to stop him. Why kill two in the open and the last one by the bayou? Could it be he knew her and didn't want her body found right away?

As Mike drove back to the police station, Hutch laid her head back against the seat. This was the first time that visiting a crime scene had left her this emotionally drained. She felt tired and old. All she wanted was a cup of coffee and a quiet room. The sun was high overhead and beat down on the car.

Mike saw how much visiting the crime scene affected Hutch this time, "Do you want to go home for a while instead?"

Hutch nodded her head yes. As soon as they entered the house, she turned on the lights. The dark bothered her lately. It probably had something to do with this case. She opened the curtains in the living room and let the afternoon sun into the tiny room.

She walked into the kitchen to find Mike brewing them a pot of coffee. The kitchen was her favorite room in the house. It was always bright and airy. There was no place for the ghosts to hide in this room. No matter how many cases she solved or how many victims she put to rest, there were always more waiting on her.

As Hutch sipped on her coffee, she told Mike, "The killer surprised the victim. She didn't expect him to kill her. I get the feeling he picked her up from the airport, but I can't be certain of that. I had a hard time reading this particular crime scene."

"Why do you think that is?"

Shrugging her shoulders, "I don't know. It was as if the evil this killer generates prevented me from seeing too much."

"This never happened to you before?"

Hutch shook her head, "No, not after a murder took place. Normally, I can picture the scene as it happens, but with this killer, it is different."

***

He woke up early, wanting to read the morning paper as soon as it was delivered. He rushed out the front door as soon as he heard it hit the ground. On the front page was the story about the recent murder. He knew the article would run; the murder was on everyone's lips yesterday.

He wondered if the news of the body would be picked up by the media across the country. When he turned on the TV, the local stations here were already airing the news this morning. He planned on searching the web to see if the news had hit the internet.

It was such a rush yesterday to be in the thick of the pandemonium he caused. He didn't like that the new detective sensed his presence. She could tell his exact location. A new plan formed in his mind. Anticipation bubbled up inside of him at the very idea of what he intended. This case was about to get even more personal for her, and she better be prepared.

Chapter 21

Gabrielle was deciding what she wanted to do tonight when the doorbell rang. Wondering who it was, she looked through the peephole and her heart swelled when she saw him, "This is a nice surprise. I figured you were busy at work."

Holding up the grocery bags, "I thought I would show off my cooking skills for you. I hope you don't mind."

Gabrielle smiled up at him, "I was just trying to decide what to do for supper. I would love for you to show me how well you can cook."

"Unless, of course, you would rather go out?"

"To tell you the truth, I have had enough of the public today. I would much rather open a bottle of wine and watch you cook. I would like to freshen up, though."

Gabrielle reached up and kissed him quickly on the lips before dashing to her room to freshen up. As she entered her room, she told him, "Make yourself at home. I won't be long."

He walked around the small house, trying to get a better feel for her. He couldn't seem to get his mind off her. Instead of hunting tonight, he felt the overwhelming need to be with her.

As he set up in the kitchen, he heard Gabrielle exit her bedroom. She took his breath away standing there in the doorway, "You look stunning."

Gabrielle blushed at the compliment. She pulled up a stool at the bar and asked, "Can I help you with something?"

He shook his head, "I have everything under control."

"This is heaven for me. I have never had a man offer to cook a meal for me before. You are spoiling me way too much."

As he cooked supper, she opened a bottle of Pinot Noir wine. "I wanted to enjoy your company as much as possible tonight. This allows me to spend all of my time with you."

She asked, "So Chef, what is on the menu tonight?"

"I thought we would splurge this evening. You will have to sit back and watch."

He took out the stock pot and placed lobsters in it. "Okay, now you are spoiling me." She told him, "I have never had lobster before."

Giving her a wicked smile, "You are in for a treat then. I managed to get some of the seafood boil Beazell's On The Bayou uses." Using his fingers, he blew a kiss, "This will be the best lobster you will ever have."

"How did you get some of their seasoning?"

Covering the pot, he took out the steaks to begin preparing them, "Let's just say, I have my sources."

She peeked into the cake box, "Oh my goodness, you do know someone there. I will definitely have to work this supper off. I love their doberge cakes. Which filling did you get?"

"Why raspberry, of course?"

She leaned back in her chair and let out a soft moan. "You can come over and cook for me any time you want, but please, you don't have to always feed me like this."

Walking over, he gave her a quick kiss on her lips, tasting the wine, "I am so glad that we finally met. I have been waiting my whole life for you."

"I am so glad you introduced yourself."

As he seared the filet mignon wrapped in bacon, he asked, "How do you like yours done?"

"Medium rare, please."

"Oh, you are indeed a woman after my heart." Maybe, just maybe, she was his soul mate.

The last thing to prepare was the haricot vert. For those, he blanched them until they were perfectly done and served a simple lemon butter drizzled on top. As she filled their wine glasses once more, he prepared two plates for them. He made sure everything was expertly arranged on the plate. "You do pay special attention to detail don't you?"

He replied, "I just want to make sure that everything is perfect for you."

He was pleased that the steak came out super tender and melt in your mouth. "This is better than any restaurant I have been too. Thank you so much for the special treat." Next she tried the lobster, drenching it in the drawn butter. "Now I wish I had tried lobster years ago. This is delicious."

The evening went by quicker than he wanted. "I don't know if I can wait until the weekend to see you again. What if I came by on Wednesday? Would you be available for supper?"

"Sure. Why don't I fix something for us to eat this time though?"

He picked up her hand and tenderly kissed it, "You don't have to do that. I can take you out to eat."

"Nonsense, it's really no problem. Don't worry, I won't give you food poisoning or anything, I promise."

At the front door, he pulled her into his arms and kissed her harder than the previous times, "Until Wednesday night then."

"I'll be counting the minutes."

"I'm not sure what time I will be over here, but it will likely be sometime after seven o'clock."

Gabrielle informed him, "I will be here. I get off work at five o'clock."

He kissed her one more time before he left. She watched as he pulled away and wished it was already Wednesday.

He had been tempted to see how much further he could get with Gabrielle, but something inside of him kept him from taking the next step in their relationship. She was the first woman he'd desired. He didn't want to scare her off. He had never been with a woman before. Everything must be perfect. Was she a virgin as well?

Chapter 22

Ledet stood in front of the murder board with Hutch right by his side. He listed everything that they knew about the killings. If only they had a suspect or at least some information on the killer.

Anxiety of the killings had diminished with the knowledge of what lay ahead. Dread moved in knowing that they couldn't stop this demented killer.

Hutch watched Ledet work. He was just as tired as her, physically and emotionally. She dreaded what would happen in the very near future. This killer had turned him into some kind of driven machine. Hell, it had done that to her as well. It happened to all cops. They threw themselves hard into their work making it difficult to have a lasting relationship. She found it a miracle that she and Mike got along as well as they did.

***

Walking into the station, he felt the urgency in the air. There was a sense of helplessness with their limitations. Ledet was uncomfortable with this particular feeling. He'd worked too hard on building a tough, professional image. If anyone found out he had these feelings, would they look at him the same way? He shook his head; no, it wouldn't help his reputation. Everyone around here knew just how serious he took this job; he was something of a perfectionist. This weakness he found hiding in his psyche frustrated him.

Something had to break and soon. They requested for patrols of the areas he'd killed in to be increased and the surrounding areas that had easy access, but the area was too large. It was merely a futile attempt to catch the killer. Years of experience told him the killer would not go back to the same place twice. Besides, the media and curious citizens were crawling all over the scenes hoping to see something. Several concerned citizens placed flowers and tiny mementos where the bodies were found as well. No, the killer would find someplace new. If only they knew where he would strike next. At least they had kept a lid on the information getting out, but it was only a matter of time before something important was leaked to the press.

***

Hutch watched as Bryant walked into the room. Bryant was an average, unassuming man who was not prone to conversation, but she needed someone to talk to, to release the tension building inside of her. He seemed surprised to see her and looked up at her with fatigue etched on his face. A half-hearted smile made its appearance on his face. She asked, "Are you okay? You seem awfully quiet."

His voice was dull as he spoke, "I'm just tired."

He had been doing this job too long. He looked at the pictures in front of them with almost no empathy, "This case is wearing on all of us."

Hutch asked, "Does Ledet work his cases with this much raw emotion?"

He nodded his head in agreement, "This case bothers him more than most. He doesn't care for men who prey on young women. He doesn't even know these women, what they were like and what their dreams, ambitions or talents were but he takes it all to heart."

For a moment, Hutch heard the hatred in his voice. It caught her by surprise. However, one couldn't help but get angry when a young woman's life ended early, discarded as if she was a piece of trash. What made her even angrier was the likelihood that he'd probably already planned his next kill.

***

When he realized Hutch was still standing right next to him, his jaw tightened, and he gritted his teeth. Who did she think she was coming in on their investigation? He forced himself to relax. He asked her, "What about you? Do you always get this involved with your cases?"

She sighed, "This is my first serial killer case. I have worked on other murder cases and plenty of high profile supernatural cases, but you can't qualify those as serial killers I guess. Although, when you stop and think about it, Joshua and Bianca were both seriously evil serial killers."

He just looked down at this woman who'd suddenly stepped into this case. Not only did she perceive herself to be some kind of psychic, but she was basically a rookie as well.

Ledet walked over to his partner and asked, "What do you have against this woman?"

Bryant popped a piece of gum in his mouth and chewed noisily for a moment, "I think she's giving us a load of crap. She is a charlatan who wants to make a name for herself in this department."

Ledet just shook his head and walked away from his partner. He knew that once Bryant got an idea into his head it was impossible to change it.

***

As Hutch headed towards her desk, she saw Mike walking in with what looked to be a large bag of po'boys. He walked up to her and gave her a kiss, "Tell Ledet and Bryant to meet us in the break room. I figured y'all could use a bite to eat."

"You are the best, honey. What would I do without you?"

She walked over to Ledet and Bryant's office, "Mike brought us lunch, and if my nose is right on the mark it is po'boys."

Bryant stretched before moving toward the door, "That sounds like a good idea to me. All I had today was coffee."

Ledet looked at the murder board once more, "I guess we do need to take a break and eat. Maybe it will help if I stepped away for a while."

When they reached the break room, Mike had the po'boys laid out for them to enjoy. She was thrilled to find that he'd brought extra *Wow Wee* Dipping Sauce to go with the fries. "I wasn't sure what everyone liked, so I had them do a combination of fish, shrimp, and oysters." He handed Hutch hers, "For you though, I have a shrimp po'boy with extra *Wow Wee* Sauce, just how you like it."

Ledet gave them a smile, "If I slept with you, would I get special treatment also?"

Hutch swatted at Ledet before tearing open the wrapper to her po'boy and digging in. Mike smiled over at Ledet, "I am open on Thursdays if you are interested man."

Ledet let out a loud laugh, forgetting how good it felt to laugh every once in a while. "Nah, I don't like to share and something tells me neither does that woman of yours."

With a mouth full of succulent shrimp, Hutch just shook her head before responding, "Nope, I don't share. My mom always complained that I was very rude as a child. I never once wanted to share anything I had. I guess I never did learn."

Ledet just laughed, "Yeah, well, I'm not sure if I could take waking up to that ugly mug of yours Mike. I don't know how Hutch here does it."

This time it was Mike's turn to laugh, "You and me both, mon ami. I am a lucky man and will be happy when I can have her back full time. Guy is a great partner, but not near as pretty as Hutch in the looks department."

***

Hutch grimaced when she noticed that it was almost ten o'clock at night. She leaned back in her chair and tried to stretch the kinks out. She rested her head on her desk and closed her eyes. Today had been a long day. She was ready to go home, take a nice hot bath and curl up in Mike's arms.

A loud crash of thunder resonated through the building. The storm they'd predicted had made its way here. As she unlocked her purse from her drawer, the strangest feeling of being watched came over her. She listened to see if she heard anything, but only silence greeted her.

She shrugged off the sensation and made her way to the door. As she passed the break room, she was certain she heard someone. She peeked into Ledet's office to find him busy at work, "I'm going home. Is anyone else around?"

"No, we are the only poor saps left. The night shift may be lurking about somewhere, but I haven't seen them."

"Okay. Well then I will see you tomorrow."

As she left the homicide department, she heard footsteps behind her. This time she knew she wasn't being paranoid. Once again, there was no one there. She swore, though, that someone watched her from the shadows. Not wanting to linger and find out who it was, she made a dash for her car.

Chapter 23

The young woman opened the motel room door as the taxi driver carried her luggage in for her. She reached into her purse to pay him just as she caught sight of him closing the door. The room was suddenly bathed in darkness. She fumbled for the light switch. Illusive shadows danced across the room as panic set in. Before she had a chance to ask him why he closed the door, she felt the cold steel of the knife blade as it touched her neck. She never had the opportunity to scream as he slit her throat from ear to ear. Blood splattered on the wall and floor as she slumped to the floor.

He calmly picked her up and placed her on the bed so he could remove her eyes and tongue. He stared down at the body and admired his handiwork. A thin smile parted his lips as he turned and walked out of the room.

***

Hutch bolted upright in bed, drenched in perspiration. With a trembling hand, she reached out to touch Mike, needing to feel him next to her for comfort. Hutch looked around the room to make sure no ghosts waited for her to wake up. Thankfully, all she saw was the familiar outline of the furniture. Moonlight made its way through the shades hanging in the window. It was too early to be awake. She had a busy day ahead of her and needed to go back to bed. If her dream was correct, she would be getting another call soon about another body having been found.

She looked down at Mike as he slept peacefully beside her, emitting an occasional snore that broke the eerie silence in the room.

Her heart stopped for a moment. She thought she heard a noise from somewhere in the room. Her auditory senses were on full alert now, listening for strange noises. She let out a sigh of relief when silence greeted her.

Her gaze darted around the room looking for anything different lurking about in the shadows. She made out Mike's clothes as they dangled from the arm of the chair. He had been too tired last night to do anything more than toss them onto the chair before curling up into bed. They both were worn out. Everything in the room seemed to be in order.

She slipped out of bed and made her way to the kitchen. Turning on the single cup coffee pot, she waited for the water to warm up. She slumped against the bar for a long moment before sliding herself onto one of the bar stools.

Still unable to relax, her body quivered with uncontrollable jitters crawling up her spine. She poured herself a cup of coffee and waited for its warmth to calm her. Her racing heart slowed down as she sipped her coffee.

A movement caught her attention as Mike stumbled into the kitchen, "What's wrong?"

"I had another dream."

He came over and pulled her into his warm embrace. She felt herself relaxing even more as his strong arms wrapped around her. "Come on, let's go back to bed."

Hutch let him lead her into the bedroom. Once she was in bed, she continued to replay the dream in her head. All she could do was wait for her phone to ring.

Hutch was surprised to find that it was the sound of her alarm and not her phone that woke her. Could it be that last night was simply a nightmare? She turned on the morning news as she dressed.

The clamor of breaking news stopped her dead in her tracks. A reporter stood outside a hotel in Baton Rouge trying to get the attention of every official at the scene, hoping that one of them would talk to her. "I am standing in front of a local hotel here in Baton Rouge where a grisly murder took place sometime during the night. This morning, a young housekeeper found a body; however, the local police have not released any details of the incident."

Panic squeezed the air from her lungs as she looked over the scene in front of her. She felt her knees buckle as she realized that the killer did strike again last night, but this time it was in Baton Rouge and not New Orleans. This case would be multi-jurisdictional now.   There was a chance that the FBI would be brought in. She hoped they could convince the detectives in Baton Rouge to hold off before bringing in the FBI. She hated to have them get involved in the case and learn about her abilities. Up until now, she was able to keep her "abilities" hidden, but the FBI had ways of finding out information that didn't concern them.

She was so engrossed in the news that she didn't hear Mike come in the room, "Now we know why your phone didn't ring last night."

Hutch nodded her head in agreement, "It looks as if our killer moved on."

"No, if the killer is indeed a taxi driver then he more than likely picked up his fare and killed her once he got her to where she was going. We are looking for a cab driver that works the airport."

"You may be right. It will be like looking for a needle in a haystack though. Nothing says the killer is a legit taxi driver. Drivers are constantly being busted for operating without the necessary licenses."

Hutch thought about what Mike said, "I wish I could get a clearer picture of his car or at least him. In my visions, he appears to be driving a black taxi cab, but I have been unable to locate very many registered black taxi cabs."

"Each vision gives you a little more. Hopefully it won't be long before you see enough to find out who the killer is."

On the ride to work, Hutch thought about the killer and last night's vision. She needed to call Baton Rouge first thing to inform them that their killer struck before in New Orleans.

Her mind kept flashing back to the murder. The victim was caught off guard. The killer did what he intended to do and then left. He showed no sign of remorse. He had been cool, calm and collected. He removed the eyes and tongue with the precision of a surgeon.

Chapter 24

Hutch blinked her eyes a few times and looked around. The visions had become frequent and more vivid. She was drawn into the vision which made her uncomfortable. Thankfully, this time she was at home. She looked down to find herself in the kitchen with her hands grasping the edge of the counter so hard her knuckles were white. Sighing, she went to push a strand of hair behind her ear to find that her hands were actually trembling.

She closed her eyes once more and took in a deep, calming breath. She wished the women would show her their killer's face.

She stepped over to the sink and rinsed her hands under the cool water and brought some to her face. As she dried her hands and face, she tried to recall the vision. Thankfully, when the vision hit she was pouring a cup of coffee and not cutting vegetables or worse, driving. If she didn't get a grip on these visions soon, there was a chance she could end up getting hurt. When she had a vision her body became frozen in place, but would that always be the case? One time she drove to where Rayne was murdered just to talk to her. Would that happen again? She may have to tell Mike exactly what was happening to her so that he could stop her from sleep walking.

She walked over to her briefcase and pulled out her notebook. She recorded every detail of the visions just in case she forgot an important detail. Taking her time, she wrote down everything she remembered. She described every detail, even going as far as any sounds or smells she recalled.

She sipped her coffee as she tried to calm herself. Still feeling uneasy, she walked over to the window. She peered out into the yard. The sun started to rise.

Hutch tried to center herself and really concentrate, searching for the source of the dark emotions. Was the killer nearby or far away?

Breathing shallowly, she pulled images out of the maelstrom in her mind. The colors of the energy were so dark that she feared the killer was very near, but every time she pictured him, his aura was dark. If only she could get a clearer image of him.

Chapter 25

Gabrielle stopped by Beazell's On The Bayou on the way home to pick up the shrimp etouffee, boneless stuffed chicken and a bourbon pecan pie she'd ordered for tonight's supper. This was the perfect meal for them. She had everything ready at the house for the green salad and even a bottle of Sangria chilling.

She stopped by the bakery and picked up a fresh loaf of bread. Her car smelled so good that her mouth watered.

Once at home, she had just enough time to put everything in the oven to keep it warm while she took a quick shower. She couldn't wait for him to get here. She enjoyed having him here. It was a more intimate setting, and she had a better chance to get closer to him. She hoped to convince him to stay the night.

As she finished dressing, the doorbell rang. "Just a minute."

She rushed to the door to welcome him. She was surprised to find him holding a single red rose and a sheepish grin.

"Your neighbor may come after me. I was in such a rush to get here I didn't stop by the store to pick up something."

She reached up and kissed him, "I think a fresh picked flower is more romantic than anything you could have bought. I still can't figure out why some woman hasn't snatched you up before now."

"I'm just unlucky in love I guess or maybe that is lucky."

She laughed, "All I know is it is good luck on my part. Come on in. I have to confess that I cheated on supper. The only thing I made was the green salad, and that came from a bag. The actual meal itself came from Beazell's On The Bayou."

For a moment, she thought his voice sounded strained as he said, "Sounds perfect to me. It smells delicious too."

She informed him, "I have a bottle of Sangria chilling in the fridge if you want to open it. I'll fix us a plate. Would you prefer to dine al fresco or sit in the dining room?"

"It's a beautiful night; let's eat outside."

"That sounds good to me." Gabrielle set their plates on the patio table while he opened the wine.

He brought them each a glass of wine to the table. "It smells delicious."

Over dinner, she spoke about how her day went as he listened. She noticed that ever since his arrival, he seemed to be quieter than normal.

They moved to the swing to finish the wine and enjoy their dessert. The moon and stars shined brightly helping to give the night a romantic atmosphere.

She sat down on the swing and curled her legs under her. He came to sit next to her. Her knee touched his thigh, and it sent tiny electrical currents through her body.

She was falling in love with him the more they talked and spent time together. She couldn't stop wondering what it would be like to have his arms wrapped around her. Just thinking about kissing him sent a shiver down her spine. She forced herself not to let her eyes travel further down his body.

She was so engrossed in her private thoughts about him that she didn't hear what he said, "I'm sorry my mind must have drifted off."

"I was just saying that it's getting late; unfortunately, I have to be at work early in the morning. I should get going."

She hid her disappointment that he couldn't stay longer. Moving in closer, she touched her lips to his. She hoped she didn't scare him off by being bold, "You could stay here tonight if you want."

***

As soon as she spoke the words, his mother's voice echoed through his mind, "I told you she was a hussy. She is a slut just like the others."

"I appreciate the offer, but I really must get going; besides, I don't want to impose."

She followed him to the door. "Thanks again for dinner."

"Thank you so much for coming. I enjoy your company."

He leaned down and kissed her. As she wrapped her arms around his neck and pulled him in closer, the kiss deepened. He pulled her closer to his body. She melted against him.

Her touched ignited something deep inside of him. He battled with his conscience and his mother's nagging. He shouldn't get involved with her until he found out more about her; however, the longer they kissed the harder it became for him to walk away tonight. Right now, he was tempted to throw it all away and drag her off to the bedroom. Fear kept him from doing this. Would she laugh at him when she found out he didn't know how to please a woman? What if she was more promiscuous than he believed?

"I better let you get to bed before this goes any further."

***

She wanted to ask him to stay, but she found it difficult to find her voice. She couldn't stand the humiliation of rejection again if he said no. Her body trembled with desire for him.

As soon as he left, she felt cold from where his body had been. She missed his arms wrapped tightly around her. She wanted him to stay, but the words never made it out of her mouth.

As he drove away, she waited until she no longer saw his taillights before closing the door. She hoped he changed his mind and turned back, taking her straight to the bedroom. When she realized that wasn't going to happen, she locked the door.

Her body still ached for him; it was going to be a long night. Her mind was still reeling. She wasn't used to a guy keeping things from moving too fast. Could he be too good to be true?

Knowing that she would not sleep until she found some relief, she went to her room and put on her outfit. Tonight she wanted to be the Dominatrix and planned to have a man satisfy her every need. It may be wrong, but something deep inside of her craved this. After he had left, she needed to find relief.

Chapter 26

Ledet let out a long sigh as he sat back at his desk with yet another cup of coffee. He took a sip and grimaced as the bitter coffee hit his taste buds. He should have gone out for a cup, but there never seemed to be any time lately. This case was everyone's top priority, but there wasn't anything to go on.

Most of the officers went back to working other duties. They needed more evidence to allow them to continue. Ledet input information regarding the murders in the computer, but nothing came back that helped them. There was just no evidence.

Several retired officers offered their time. They helped monitor the bayous and combed through the swamplands hoping to stumble upon something, anything to help them.

They received several calls from people swearing they saw something. Every lead was followed up on, but the end result remained the same, nothing. He despised the calls from pitiful individuals desperately trying to glorify their name through this case. If they only knew that each tip or potential lead had to be followed up on, and these calls wasted their resources and their time.

The thought of having to work another crime scene seemed to drain what little energy Ledet had left. He did his job well, as did his partners, but he felt as if he weren't doing enough. In his gut though, he knew they would investigate more crime scenes until they finally stopped this killer. If they were unable to stop him, New Orleans would be turned into a bloody killing field where no brown haired, brown eyed woman would be safe. Unfortunately, well over half the women in New Orleans fit that description.

Chapter 27

Deep in the night, a man intent on evil watched the woman of his dreams. He recorded her every move this last week. Every night he sat outside her house, not moving a muscle. Content waiting to find out if she was truly his soulmate.

Now that he knew the answer, he would see that she joined the others. His mother assured him she would take good care of this whore. His blood coursed through his body in anticipation of spilling her blood.

His palms grew sweaty, and his heart pounded in his chest as the thrill of the kill took over his body.

***

The music that filled the club vibrated through her body as she made her way to the dance floor. It had been over a week since she heard from him. Gabrielle probably scared him off by being so brazen. She let her inner personality show through a little too much for him.

This was where she came to be her true self. She could let her hair down and party. Here, she had complete freedom to be whoever she wanted. More importantly, no one knew who she was.

The bar was extremely busy tonight. She was anxious to go wild on the dance floor and be whisked away by a guy for a night of hot sex. It was so much fun the other night as the dominatrix that tonight she wanted to be a submissive. She watched in utter anticipation as a handsome man made his way to her. He was a little older than what she generally went for, but she found him intriguing. It could be the way he carried himself, almost as if he could care less if anyone paid attention to him. It was as if he would rather just blend in than stand out.

He came over and asked, "You want to dance?"

Instead of answering, she simply wrapped her arms around his neck and gave him a full body kiss. She wanted to dance with this man, but not on the dance floor. She had something more intimate in mind.

As soon as they turned into the alleyway, she pushed him against the cold brick wall and kissed him hard. At first she wanted to be the submissive, but now, she wanted to be the one in control.

As the kiss deepened, she thought about how exciting this was. She was kissing a man who she didn't know. As the thrill of the moment took over, she was unable to think of anything else. She planned on completely losing herself in the heat of the moment.

She smiled up at him and asked, "Did you like that?"

Instead of answering, he twirled her around to where she was the one up against the brick wall. Her partner never had a chance to defend himself before the knife struck deep in his back. It made a sluicing sound as it was pulled out.

Before her foggy mind could realize something was terribly wrong, it was too late. Everything happened in slow motion. It was as if she watched what was going on from afar. Sinister orbs glowed from the dark shadow of a man. Fear paralyzed her.

Standing in front of her was the man she thought she loved. His face distorted in a mask of rage. The eyes staring down at her were as cold as ice.

She didn't even see the flash of the blade as he brought it up against her neck. Her body quickly turned cold as the blood poured from the huge gash in her neck.

She looked down at her body slumped there in a contorted position. She tried to scream as the man pushed her hair out of the way and stared down at her face with a malicious sneer. She couldn't bear to watch as he mutilated her face. She couldn't even fathom the thought that she was murdered. Suddenly, whispers surrounded her, welcoming her into their fold. She told herself this wasn't real, it was a nightmare.

***

Hutch knew a call this early in the morning meant only one thing, another murder. Without bothering with makeup, she threw her hair into a haphazard ponytail and dressed. After slipping on her tennis shoes, she headed out the door.

She made it to the crime scene before the other detectives. She was already dodging several reporters who'd made it here before Ledet and Bryant. What was keeping the two men? Ledet usually arrived before either of them.

A pair of headlights closing in on the crime scene announced Ledet's arrival. He looked disheveled tonight, which was highly unlike him. Something about his intense glare hardened his handsome features and distorted them into something fearful. It worried her to see him like this.

She was at least grateful that he arrived before Bryant. There was no denying the intense dislike Bryant felt for her. It radiated off of him even though he tried to hide it.

In the background, she heard one of the other officers mentioning that Hutch must have had another vision about a dead body. She wasn't sure how anyone found out about her abilities, but she hoped they kept it quiet. This didn't need to be leaked to the press.

Hutch was unsure if this poor woman was killed by the same man. The MO was all wrong. A man and woman were killed. Besides, Hutch never had a vision to announce this murder.

Even now, she could not pick up any vibes. She closed her eyes to get a feel for what happened here. Darkness closed in around her, and she stepped inside of it. She let the images float around her, waiting for them to come into focus, but nothing happened. She did not see anything.

As she was about to give up, a sharp image shot through the darkness. It disappeared before she could make out the image. It was as if the killer didn't want her to read this scene. How was that possible? This gift should come with an instruction manual, something short and to the point. She had to seek Rayne out later on to see if she knew if this poor woman and man had joined the others.

Chapter 28

Mike sipped his Beazell's Bloody Mary and looked over at Hutch one more time. He could not keep his eyes off of her tonight. Aware of his lingering stare, she looked up and gave him one of her dazzling smiles. He couldn't help but feel protective toward this woman he loved with all his heart.

***

Hutch felt Mike's eyes roam slowly, yet deliberately, over her. She saw the desire in his eyes and felt the heat emitting from his body. She reached over and grabbed his hand in hers.

The waiter appeared to be extremely nervous tonight as he asked, "Have you decided what you would like from the menu?" Hutch noticed how he continued to fidget with his tie and shifted his weight from one foot to another. What was bothering him tonight? She tried to get a sense of what he was feeling, but he had put up a barricade around himself. She found that strange. After dealing with this case, she found everyone's actions strange, no matter how small they were. She found herself paying attention to the aura around men as she attempted to decipher if they were their killer just by the energy surrounding them.

She looked up at the waiter one more time and gave him a smile, "I will have the same as Mike." The Beazell House Nicoise Salad with a light herb vinaigrette sounded perfect for tonight. She wasn't in the mood for anything heavy, and this would hit the spot. The nicoise salad served here was a heavenly combination of hard-boiled eggs, grilled shrimp, potatoes, olives, and green beans. It was like a well composed orchestra for your mouth. Everything she ate here had been well prepared and seasoned to perfection. The food tantalized your taste buds and satisfied your soul. Unlike most of the other restaurants here in New Orleans, the food wasn't overly salty and not so spicy that you couldn't taste the food.

As she handed him her menu, their hands briefly touched. In that split second, an aura of darkness shrouded her. She swallowed hard to help shake the feeling and took in a deep breath.

Mike sensed a change in her, "Are you okay honey?"

She just nodded her head, "Yeah, I am fine." When she looked up, the waiter was gone. She wondered why she'd had such a strong reaction to a simple touch.

As they waited for their food, Hutch dove into the house butter flavored with oranges and the Beazell's House Seasoning. She couldn't seem to get enough of this stuff. It beat honey butter by a landslide. As she enjoyed her bread and butter, she let her eyes roam the restaurant. She needed to stop this bad habit, but once again, she hoped to see an aura around someone here that would lead her to the killer.

As the waiter placed the Beazell House Nicoise Salad in front of them, Hutch dug in. The sight of the crisp, fresh salad and shrimp grilled to perfection made her realize just how hungry she was. Whereas Mike preferred to eat everything separately, she preferred the combination of flavors as they danced in her mouth. The vinaigrette was sheer perfection. It not only brought out all the wonderful delicate flavors of the food but somehow enhanced them. The chef here was a culinary master. The shrimp in the salad awakened her taste buds. The seasoning on the shrimp was over the top scrumptious.

As Hutch enjoyed her food, she was glad they'd stopped to eat before going home. The food here was a magical cure for her. The stress left her body with each bite of food. Yes, this place was indeed the perfect place for supper tonight. It gave her a break from the case. She practically worked around the clock on the murders and needed a break.

Mike and Hutch were walking back to their car after supper when suddenly the wind seemed to have a bite to it. The sky around her turned gray as a mist swirled around her. She had grabbed for Mike's hand before she lost herself in the vision.

She heard the water as it made its way to the river bank. Without looking into the water, she knew that a victim was there, waiting to be found. She was caught on the bony branches in the water. The body moved in an unnatural rhythm that only the dead danced to when submerged in the murky water. The river rushed around her as if she belonged there.

In this vision, she did not witness the actual murder, just where her body was. Around her, she sensed the fear that radiated throughout the night air. The woman's screams were lost in the hollow, empty night as he slit her throat with complete ease.

He had killed once again. He was never satisfied, always needing to kill another woman. Hutch stood in the shadows, frozen in fear, and watched as the scene played out before her. There was nothing she could do.

Hutch looked around, hoping this time she saw his face. The moon was bright with beams filtering through the trees, leaving dark, sinister shadows. Instinctively, she backed into the darkness when she heard a noise up near the river. He was there, waiting and watching, but for what? Did he know she was here?

Suddenly, he turned around and looked right at her. She felt his eyes staring straight into her eyes. That couldn't be. There was no way he could somehow cut through her vision and see her. Then again, she could make out his shape so was there a chance he saw her too? If only his appearance would be clearer, but as usual, it was nothing more than a black shape. All she saw was his aura.

The next thing she saw was the killer smiling at her before disappearing into the night.

***

As the wind viciously blew through the alley, Hutch opened the black body bag that was placed over the victim. Dr. Ortego wanted to preserve as much evidence as he could and upon his arrival immediately secured the body as best as he could. With the wind blowing the way it was, there was no telling how much debris had blown in after the murder or what evidence may have blown away.

The poor dead girl was only twenty-one. Her friends had noticed her missing from the club and started to search for her. What they found would never leave any of their minds and showed them the dangers of leaving a bar with someone you don't know.

She took in a sharp breath. The very essence of death still hung heavy in the air. She swore once more as she looked at the body. She felt the young girl's presence still here in the alley. The young girl appeared right before her dead body. There was such sorrow and despair in the air that Hutch had a hard time reading the scene. The young girl stated, "All I wanted to do was to let my hair down for once, have some fun and not think about consequences."

There was so much that Hutch could tell her about the dangers of those actions, but unfortunately she learned the hard way about the dangers of those actions.

Hutch attempted to get a feel for the scene. As her hair continued to whip her face from the forceful wind, she reached into her pocket and grabbed a scrunchy. Once she secured her hair, she made her way back to the club. Maybe if she walked the same path as the girl, she would get a better feel for the killer.

As she neared the bar, she noticed that this particular area was deserted. The echoing sound of her heels was the only noise she heard. The crime scene seemed far away when in actuality it was just right around the corner. Even if the woman had screamed, she doubted anyone would have heard her.

As soon as she arrived at the bar, she began to get a feel for the area at night. An approaching vehicle caught her attention. She said a quick prayer as the coroner's van passed by her.

She watched as shadows danced across the sidewalk as she attempted to put herself in the killer's footsteps. A cold breeze blew through her, causing her to look up at the sky. She loved watching the sun rise. It reaffirmed her belief that a new day was here, full of new potentials. That gave her hope that this may be the day they caught this killer.

She took a moment to enjoy the onset of morning as the sun's rays penetrated the darkness of the night. Ledet walked over to her. She put up her finger to her lips and whispered, "Don't say a word." She surveyed the area.

Ledet could tell something was bothering her, "What's wrong?"

"I just had an overwhelming sensation that someone was watching me."

"Do you know from where?"

Hutch shook her head, "No, I couldn't tell where the vibes were coming from." Looking around once more, "Maybe it was just a shadow."

As she tried to brush off the feeling of being watched, it was still very strong. As they walked to the crime scene, Hutch felt as if she was suddenly transported to hell. She felt herself teetering between the real world and the ghoulish nightmare of the vision. Even if she wanted to extricate herself from this place, her focus remained on what she saw and felt. Her heart pounded as hands roamed over her body; no wait, she was in the victim's body. The hands roaming over her body were ice cold, as cold as his eyes.

She heard Bryant's loud mouth in the background, "Is she all right?" Nothing could break the hypnotic spell she was under. Her body trembled as the cold steel of the knife moved across her throat. She watched as the shadows moved in, "He's close."

With that one sentence, Hutch was brought back to reality. Her surroundings came back into focus, and the sounds normalized. She shook her head to clear her jumbled thoughts. A piercing thought entered her mind, "I can get to you anytime and anywhere, remember that."

She turned to Ledet and informed him, "He is near; I am sure of it. We have to make sure the crime scene techs get pictures of everyone here and then we need to compare them with the photos of the other scenes to see who was at each scene."

Ledet looked around, "Are you sure he is here?"

"I am positive. He is very close." Hutch paid close attention to all the bystanders in close proximity hoping to pick up a dark shadow or aura hanging over them. She let out a few mumbled curses before moving on.

A shiver of fear ran through her as she thought about the message that penetrated her mind. It was as if he could get into her head. This was merely a game to him.

***

He watched her through veiled eyes. He clenched his hands tightly as she walked the scene. It took all of his willpower not to continue taunting her, but it was too dangerous. There was a chance that it would backfire, and she would turn right towards him and see his true self. He watched earlier when the souls had cried out to her to be careful. It was a thrill to be this near and her not know.

Chapter 29

The two bodies lay in the bayou a few feet apart. One was bloated and grotesque looking. Decomposition had already started while the newer body had only been in the water a short while.

The older body had lost all distinguishable characteristics. Fish, and more than likely some carnivores, already started to eat the body, but the newest body remains were untouched. Her face still showed the anguish of the terror she'd suffered. It was twisted into a grotesque mask that showed her final minutes of life.

The man stood over the bodies, frozen in fear. His mouth silently moved in terror as his eyes surveyed the grisly scene in front of him. The scream caught in his throat. It could not be forced out. He stood frozen in place. His eyes refused to shut out the nightmare in front of him. His breathing stopped, and his rapid heartbeat thundered in his ears. His fingers went numb and lost their grip on the rifle he held. He never even heard the thud as it hit the ground near him.

Suddenly, his brain pieced together what he saw. He felt the bile rise in his throat. The air became thick and closed around him.

A noise behind him shook him out of his reverie. The sound of his son's approaching footsteps brought him to action.

He hollered back at his son, "Owen stay there. Don't come any closer." He planned to take his son duck hunting for the first time, but it looked as if their plans for the day were ruined. As he looked at the bodies, though, he realized at least he still had his son. Some parents were about to learn their daughters weren't coming home. He said a quick novena over the bodies and made the sign of the cross before ushering his son back to the truck. Taking out his cell phone, he called the police to report what he'd found and made sure that his son was secure in the vehicle before giving the grisly details. He kept his gun ready to fire in case the killer was still lurking about, but from the look of the bodies, he was long gone.

As soon as he got back into the truck, Owen asked, "What's wrong Dad? Aren't we going hunting? Did work call?"

He shook his head, "No son. There is something in the water. I had to call the police. We need to wait for them before we can leave, though, okay?"

Owen, being a curious twelve year old, "Cool, can I go see what it is? Is it an alligator that someone shot? Come on Dad. Let's go look one more time."

Grabbing the door handle before Owen could open the door, "No son, this isn't something that you should see. It's something that no one ever needs to see."

***

The dispatcher drew in a deep breath before calling Ledet, "A hunter found two bodies in the bayou sir. He and his son were going out duck hunting this morning when he stumbled upon the bodies. At least he told his son to stay back until he checked the area for alligators and such. One appears to have been there for a bit, but the other one looks as if she was just placed there."

Ledet replied "Get the crew out there as soon as possible. Please ask that hunter to stay there until we get there."

"That is already done, sir. What about Detective Hutcherson?"

"I will call her. Get the rest of the team out the door, please?"

As he hung up the phone, he waited as the news spread over him. He called Hutch to let her know what was going on.

Even though traffic was light at this hour, it still took him half an hour to get to the crime scene. As he climbed out of his car, he saw what could only be the father's truck. They assumed they would be enjoying a quiet morning of hunting and instead their peaceful morning was ruined. The father would never view the world the same again. He would think twice about heading to the bayou again. You never knew what you may find floating in the water.

Beyond the ferns and cypress trees fringing the bayou lay the bodies that washed up from the bayou. They were still partially submerged in the dark, murky water. The smell of death hung heavy in the air. It would be a while before he could get the smell out of his nose.

Ledet introduced himself to the father as the son stayed in the car, playing games on his dad's phone. Ledet agreed that was for the best. The child didn't need to hear what his father had to say. After he had taken statements and any necessary information, Ledet sent the father and son back home.

By the time they had left, Bryant had arrived. Hutch was still walking the scene. As he headed to the water's edge to observe the bodies further, images of the previous crime scenes flashed through his mind. One look confirmed that this was the handiwork of their killer.

A flurry of activity took place around them as crime scene techs gathered evidence and took pictures. Dr. Ortego examined both bodies before removing them.

A haze settled over the bayou this morning. Summer had returned with a vengeance. It gripped you by the throat and squeezed with a viciousness. Barely eight o'clock and it was already ninety degrees outside. Dr. Ortego wiped the back of his neck with his handkerchief before tending to the bodies. Most would fault the heat and humidity for the discomfort here at the crime scene. They all knew the heat wasn't to blame for the suffocating pall. No, that was not it. Evil had settled over this area once again. It spread its tentacles of malice like a silent cancer taking hold of the unsuspecting body.

Dr. Ortego barked out orders. "David, put on your waders. You need to get in the water to help with the retrieval. We have to be extremely careful when we move the body. Let's try to get the body bag underneath before picking it up." Dr. Ortego turned to Ledet, "It will take all of us to lift the body. We can't just pick it up not knowing exactly how long it has been in the water. We want to avoid as much slippage as possible."

Ledet shuddered at the thought. It took some maneuvering to get the body bag under the body. It was heavier than he thought, and the smell became worse now that it was moved. They proceeded to do the same thing with the other body, even though decomposition hadn't started on the poor lady.

As Ledet looked over the crime scene, he pondered his choice of career. He dealt with human trash on a daily basis and had to witness such sweet innocence destroyed by monsters bent on making sure their sick desires were satisfied.

His heart constricted at the thought of telling not one but two families about their loss. One body wasn't able to be identified by sight. It would take a while to identify her.

Chapter 30

He was careful to slip through the police station while everyone was busy with shift changes and finishing their reports for the day. A sinister smile formed across his face as he thought of how easy it had been to fool these imbeciles.

He watched the file room waiting for the opportune moment. He saw it when the receptionist left the room. Moving quickly, he slipped in before the door closed.

He looked down at his watch to see that he had been searching through files for over two hours with no luck yet. He wanted to find anything the department may have on Detective Grace Hutcherson.

She was fairly new to the New Orleans Police Department and her previous employer had only forwarded the pertinent information. There was nothing in here that helped him regarding her "psychic abilities" she claimed to possess.

It made little sense that her abilities were progressing, and she had started to get to him. He had been haunted with these abilities all of his life, but he never told anyone of his capabilities. They would probably treat him as an outcast just as his mother had.

***

Hutch's mind tried to move through the muddled exhaustion of her brain, but everything seemed to short circuit. She was so tired. She pushed the papers away from her desk and decided to go home and wait for Mike.

Hutch was not in the mood to cook so she stopped to pick them up a pizza before getting some much needed sleep. She'd spent her day looking over the files and had found little useful information.

Before leaving, she walked over to Ledet's desk to tell him she was leaving. Bryant left earlier stating he had a date tonight and needed a break from the case. She couldn't blame him there. She was thankful she had Mike to help her get through the monstrosities of this case.

With each step she made, her legs felt as if they were filled with lead. The thought of going to bed sounded heavenly.

She found Ledet sound asleep at his desk. She gently shook his shoulder to wake him.

Ledet woke up with a start. He looked around to find that he was still at his desk. Hutch stared down at him, "I hated to wake you, but I figured you would be more comfortable in your own bed instead of at your desk."

Rubbing his face, "I guess you are right. You're going home as well?"

"Yes. I have to get some rest. My mind doesn't want to cooperate anymore."

Ledet stated, "I won't be able to sleep. As soon as I get home, I will pace the floor thinking of this case. I am always like this when I work these types of cases. You go home and rest, though. At least you have someone waiting at home for you."

As he turned his attention back to the mounds of paperwork on his desk, she couldn't help but feel sorry for him. He was right; at least she had Mike in her life. Before leaving, she told him, "Please try to get some rest. You won't do us any good if you are so exhausted you can't function. You and I both know I am right."

***

As Ledet was deciding if he should leave for the day, he heard a light knock on the door. When he saw the dispatcher's face, he felt his stomach tighten as he waited for the news. He felt hollow and sick. Another young woman's life had been cut too short. His whole body dulled as the sick feeling turned to nothing. There was no emotion left in his body. It was as if he had been too anesthetized to feel anything.

He picked up the phone and called Hutch. She'd just left to get some rest, and he had to drag her back.

Chapter 31

He walked in the shadows, calmly and deliberately, knowing it was impossible for him to be seen. He kept his face hidden beneath the brim of his hat. He always dressed in dark clothes. His knife moved against his ribs as he walked. It kept perfect rhythm with his movements as if they were in sync.

The kill would be quick this time. Today, he would only take what he needed. He would prove to his mother that he was the one in control.

***

Hutch was exhausted, mentally and physically. Just the thought of sleep was a luxury right now. It seemed like years since she'd had a good night's sleep. The car hummed hypnotically, and she settled into it more comfortably. She felt under a spell right now and drifted off to sleep.

She forced herself awake once more. Mike replied, "Go to sleep if you want. I will wake you up when we get there."

She shook her head, "No, I have to stay awake and get a feeling for this guy. Maybe watching the scenery will help me get better insight into him. He had to come this way. I won't be able to get any rest until he is stopped."

She looked out the window at the all too familiar sights. The first light of morning broke over the bayou. The sky was alive with various colors of pinks, grays and oranges. God could not have created a more breathtaking sunrise. If she weren't going to another murder scene she probably would find joy in watching it.

She looked at the foliage and saw the leaves changing color dramatically. Fall would soon be here. Soon this land would be scarred and naked with winter, but for now, it was breathtaking with the colors of autumn. The window to enjoy the colors of fall was short lived, and fall was normally one of her favorite seasons. Maybe she and Mike could take a ride to Virginia and enjoy the fall colors there. It would be a nice break or better yet, they could rent a little cabin on the Blue Ridge Parkway and enjoy the peace and quiet it had to offer. She didn't need a long vacation, just a couple of days away.

As they got closer to the crime scene, she felt her insides tighten. His presence still lingered here. The air was charged with his negative energy. The consuming power of his presence overwhelmed her suddenly. She told Mike, "He will be in the crowd. We aren't even there yet, and I sense him close by." By the time they arrived at the crime scene, her senses were on fire. She looked around to see if she could pick up on his location. Not seeing anything, she let out a sigh. He was nearby.

She turned her attention toward the actual crime scene. She still couldn't get over how exact her visions were. Everything was just how she saw it. The sun made its way further up in the sky, giving the area an eerie feel as the fog rose from the bayou. At any other time, Hutch would stop to take in the beauty around her, but that was shattered now. All she saw around her was death and despair.

She halted abruptly catching Mike off guard. Mike followed her eyes and realized she was staring at something ahead of them.

Hutch caught a movement in the tall grass. At first, she thought it was a gentle breeze that caused the tall grass to wave. Then her eyes came to rest on an image watching them make their way to the bayou. The image didn't look like the killer's normal black shadow. No, Hutch had a feeling it was the ghost of the young woman whose body was waiting for her. She was more than likely afraid to leave the area, unsure of where to go or what to do.

Hutch walked over to where she saw the apparition and let the morning air speak to her. A gentle breeze blew through her hair and whispered in her ear. The woods told their secrets in her ear in hushed voices. All around her, fallen leaves fluttered across the ground like small woodland creatures.

Hutch took a deep breath and slowly, almost painfully, lowered her eyes to look at the body. Her fears were confirmed. Her vision was correct once again. Her mind already knew what she would see, but it was still a shock to her system. She stood there and let the energy around her tell its story. She could smell death in the air. The young woman had only been dead a few hours. Her face was forever frozen in the pain and terror that filled her last minutes on earth.

Hutch made her way back to the car as the chaos around her continued. More police cars arrived along with a few more media vans. The crime scene technicians were still busy collecting evidence. Dr. Ortego's team prepared the body for removal and transport back to the morgue for an autopsy. She still couldn't shake the feeling that the killer was here watching them. She'd surveyed the bystanders several times now and could not locate the dark, ominous shadow that hung over him.

Ledet made his way over to her. He spoke in a monotonous voice with exhaustion clearly evident. Numbness quickly overtook what senses she had left; she needed to rest in order to face each grueling day that was sure to come her way.

He informed Hutch, "Dr. Ortego has her body now. I don't envy his job."

She nodded her head in agreement, "No, me neither."

He reached out and touched her shoulder, "I told Mike to take you home. You need to get some sleep."

She walked slowly to the car with Mike by her side. She pulled the door open and it felt heavy. The world around her suddenly seemed so unreal, like a dream. She leaned back against the seat and closed her eyes for only a moment. Her tired brain finally clicked off. There was no more thinking of death, mutilation, and monsters in the dark. Her body screamed for sleep.

Mike climbed into the driver's side and placed his hands on the steering wheel. He saw that Hutch was exhausted, "I am taking you home. You need to get some sleep. It will be a while before they have any reports for you. Let these guys do their job." She just nodded in agreement, too tired to even talk.

Hutch woke up feeling hung over. Only she didn't have one drop of alcohol, even though she needed a good stiff drink when she got home. She had been too tired to bother undressing.

She walked into the bathroom and splashed some cold water on her face. Her reflection caught her by surprise. She looked as if she had aged twenty years. In spite of sleeping a few hours, she still felt wiped out.

Flashes of images began to fill the room. She felt that horrible pit in her empty stomach open up as she saw the images of those he'd killed come before her. She felt the cold blade as it made its way across the victims' necks. They never had a chance to scream. His menacing laughter echoed in her mind.

Her emotions were dangerously close to the surface. She had to get a grip. She was a cop, and this was her job. She was accustomed to seeing death and violence. *Yeah, but you weren't used to seeing it this up close and personal.* This man cheated these families out of their loved ones. He ended all of these lives before they even had a chance to truly live.

She sat back down on the bed as her mind slowly began to focus. She went over the crime scenes once more. The images of the women followed her into the bedroom. She jumped as her cell phone rang. It was Ledet, "Hutch."

"Good, you are awake. I wanted to make sure that you got some rest. You looked drained."

"I'm feeling better than I did earlier. I am still not quite human yet though."

He let out a laugh, "I'm headed back to the office to review the files once more, but you don't have to. Stay home and get some more rest."

***

Ledet had never worked with a psychic before, but he could tell it took a lot out of her. The last thing they needed was for her to collapse and not help them with this case. She was the only connection they had with this killer.

He needed to review the files again. He couldn't shake the feeling that he was missing something, something right under his nose.

As Ledet studied the murder board, he felt a warning blaze inside of him. This guy knew what he was doing. He knew how they worked. He had to know about forensics because he had yet to leave behind any trace evidence. He knew to attack them from behind so that they couldn't scratch him. Ledet shook his head. But this couldn't be a cop. It had to be a fanatic who watched a lot of true crime television.

***

Hutch walked into the office bright and early the next morning. She was surprised to find Ledet already behind his desk reviewing files. Judging from his rumpled clothes and oily hair, he'd stayed here all night. He was unshaven and his eyes were bloodshot from lack of sleep. She wished he would go home and get some rest.

The press hounded him unmercifully and the frightened public wanted this killer behind bars now. What the press and public didn't understand was that this case took its toll on all of those working these murders. They seemed to have all aged these last few weeks. This case would more than likely leave them all with a few more emotional scars. It would be a while before any of them had a gleam back in their eyes or a smile on their face.

He looked up, and she asked, "I take it you didn't go home last night?"

He rubbed his hand over his chin, feeling the stubble, "No, I didn't. I kept going over everything in my mind. How the hell does he kill these people and not leave behind any clues?"

Chapter 32

He climbed out of bed slowly and pulled back the curtains. The sun had yet to rise. It was the perfect time to hunt. He smiled wickedly as he headed to the bathroom for a shower. He sensed his mother nearby, "Well Mother, soon I will bring another one home to join you."

He put his face under the warm, pulsating water. As he lathered the soap on his body, he let the pounding rhythm of its warmth move across his body. The room was suddenly filled with his demonic laughter.

He stepped out of the shower and toweled dry. A deep sorrow penetrated his mind, and he pushed it away. He would not feel sorry for himself. He was finally making a good life for himself.

As he dressed, he felt the others move into the room. He stated out loud, "I know you are here. There is nothing you can do. Soon I will bring another into your group. Mother, I've done this all because of you. I am saving this world by lancing infected boils such as you."

He took the electric razor and shaved, preparing for the day. He would make sure that a son never again feared the wrath of a mother like his. Pride welled up inside of him as he reminisced about everything he had accomplished.

He knew his true calling early on. He'd studied for years, poring over library books. He learned all the intricacies of how the police worked so when the time came he could ace the tests. He studied forensics and investigating. He read various books written by psychologists, learning their secrets about serial killers. He learned the common mistakes serial killers made and molded himself into the perfect killing machine, using everything he'd learned.

The police had no clue it was him killing these women. They were such fools. He doubted they would even suspect it was him doing the killings.

***

In the early morning shadows, he watched as Trinity Savoie stepped out of her tiny apartment and started her warm up exercises. A smile formed across his face as he thought of this woman and her punctuality. She was a creature of habit. She would warm up for the first ten minutes and then set out on her run.

He was impressed with her training. She was an impressive athlete, a natural. A rush of adrenaline coursed through him as he thought about what was about to happen.

He watched her start a slow jog up the street until she was out of sight. A surge of energy pulsed through him as he began his hunt. This was the first woman he had actually stalked. When he saw her on the street the other morning, he almost killed her out of impulse, but something stopped him. Instead, he just watched, observed and dreamed about the upcoming kill.

He moved to the alleyway she would soon pass through. He pulled out his knife and waited for her to pass. It would have to be quick as the morning rush hour was approaching.

He grew impatient. He feared that she had taken another route. *No, you must be patient. Fate was on your side. She will come.* He took a deep breath and waited. He listened once more for her footsteps as they hit the pavement. A rush of exhilaration moved through him as he heard her coming.

He reached out and grabbed her with no problems. He had perfected his technique, and there were no clumsy or slow movements. She was there one minute and the next minute she was gone; his hand covered her mouth, and the knife was at her throat. He'd become the perfect predator.

Before the woman became aware that evil was waiting for her, he reached out and dragged her into the dark alley. He felt her terror as she briefly struggled against him. It excited him to feel fear pulsating through her body. He was stronger and superior to her; that knowledge was even better than sex. Before she could scream in a frenzy of terror, he pressed the cold steel against her neck. He squeezed her throat for a moment and felt her freeze, but in the next instant, he slit her throat wide open.

His mother's irritating voice resonated in his head so clearly for a moment he forgot that she was dead. "You are a dirty little boy aren't you? Do the world a favor and disappear? You are nothing more than a mistake." Her cold eyes pierced right through him with complete disgust. With a surgeon's precision, her words cut out his heart. All he heard was her haunting words, "Nobody will ever love you. Nobody wants you, not even me."

His hands trembled with rage as he tried to shut out her voice. "Stop it!" he hollered out. He slashed out at the air.

He quickly removed the woman's accusing eyes and vicious tongue hoping to silence all of them.

It only took seconds to remove the eyes and tongue from his victim. His practice was paying off. Before he could complete the task with the victim's eyes, the ghosts of those he'd killed appeared. Even with him removing their eyes, he felt their stares burning into him. Wicked and menacing smiles spread across their blood streaked faces. Even without eyes, they saw him. How was that possible?

Chapter 33

"Please, you don't have to do this," Hutch fearfully called. "Don't do it. Leave her alone."

He just looked at her and smiled. He took his knife and sliced the woman's throat from ear to ear. Blood sprayed across the ground as the knife cut deep into the woman's throat. The amount of force used behind this cut almost decapitated her. The ground around her absorbed the blood as if it had an unquenchable thirst.

Hutch looked away as the killer continued his macabre work. She couldn't bear to watch the removal of the dead woman's eyes and tongue. He took such pleasure in his work.

Hutch turned toward him. Maybe she would get a good look at his face. As in the past, he was consumed by the shadows.

Hutch woke up with a jolt. Her heart grieved for the young woman whose life was cut short. Tears spilled down her cheeks. Her body shivered in grief for what she'd witnessed.

As she sat up, she was transported to another vision. This time it was something very different. Instead of witnessing the horrific scene play out, she watched the scene through the eyes of the murderer.

He walked slowly back to his car. She felt each step he made even though she was lying in bed. Suddenly, he stopped and looked back to where he'd left the body.

When he smiled, her own mouth twisted upward at the same moment.

Before he could get to his car, the vision faded away. She desperately tried to enter his mind once again. She wanted to see where he lived, get a better description of the car or anything that would be helpful. Instead, the vision ended. She lay quivering on the bed as the realization of what happened hit her. She saw through the murderer's eyes. Was this going to be something new or just a one-time event?

Mike sensed that she was awake and reached out to pull her into his embrace, "It happened again didn't it? Do you want to talk about it?"

She buried herself in the crook of his arm and swallowed hard, "Tonight, I not only watched him murder her, but for a few seconds, I saw from his eyes."

Mike sat up abruptly and brought her to him, "What do you mean? You could get into his mind?"

She nodded her head, "Yes, but only for a few seconds. Oh Mike, it was awful. I felt him walking and smiling. I experienced everything he did. That never happened before. With Joshua, I attempted to read his mind, but I never felt what he was feeling. This time, I actually felt what the murderer felt."

Mike pulled her into his arms even tighter, letting her feel his strength. She brought his head to hers and kissed him deeply. She wanted to forget about the murders and killer for a while. She wanted to feel passion and desire. Mike felt her need and he kissed her deeper. She ran her fingers through his thick hair and held him as she kissed him with raw passion. He pulled back and trailed kisses down her neck. Soon they were swept away by their passion.

Chapter 34

By the time Hutch, Ledet and Bryant arrived at the crime scene, the area was cordoned off with yellow crime scene tape. Ledet asked the young officer, "What do we have?"

"A young woman was found in the alley. From the amount of blood, this is the crime scene."

Hutch found Dr. Ortego kneeling over the body, "How bad is it?"

"Your killer struck again."

Hutch nodded her head in agreement. Her vision was correct, and the killer had hit again. Hutch squatted down and stared at the young woman. Her body lay where it fell, crumpled in a contorted heap. The only movement of the body had been the killer turning her face to remove her eyes and tongue. Hutch wondered why he didn't bother moving this body. Was someone approaching, and he didn't have time?

Ledet asked, "I wonder why he didn't move her? He didn't even take the time to pose her."

Dr. Ortego replied, "I am not sure, but it was the killer." He rolled the woman onto her back and showed them the mutilations to her face and throat.

Ledet asked Hutch, "Do you have any clue as to why he dumped and posed the last victim, but he left this one here?"

Shaking her head, "I'm not sure. I haven't been able to get a feel for this crime scene yet."

As Hutch walked the crime scene, the forensic team scoured the area for clues. She doubted that they would find much. It still bothered her that the killer didn't take the body somewhere else to pose it. Why didn't he move her? She continued to walk the crime scene, hoping to find something to use.

***

Ledet groaned when he saw the media vans arrive. He walked over to one of the young officers guarding the scene, "Make sure everyone working this case knows not to talk to the media. Let them know I will have their heads if anyone spouts off to a reporter or makes their way on the evening news. Try to keep them far away from the scene."

"Yes, sir."

Ledet pulled a packet of antacids from his pocket and popped one in his mouth. The coffee from this morning churned in his stomach suddenly. They needed to find this guy quick. The media were already all over them about this being a serial killer. Very soon, this would turn into a full three ring circus.

Chapter 35

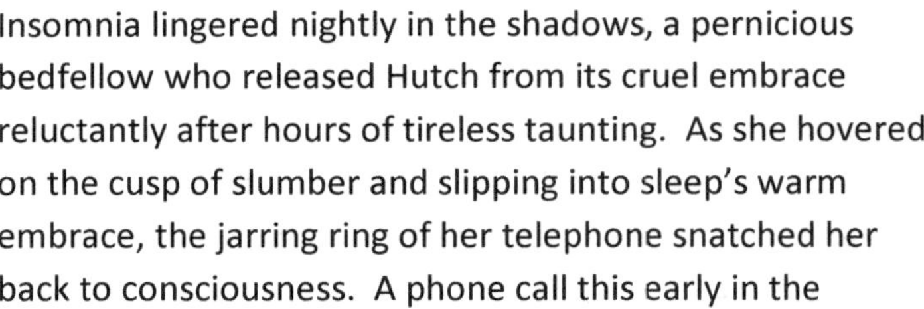

Insomnia lingered nightly in the shadows, a pernicious bedfellow who released Hutch from its cruel embrace reluctantly after hours of tireless taunting. As she hovered on the cusp of slumber and slipping into sleep's warm embrace, the jarring ring of her telephone snatched her back to consciousness. A phone call this early in the morning meant another murder took place.

"Hello."

Instead of the dispatcher's voice there was nothing but silence. She repeated, "Hello."

A chill washed over her body as she heard the voice. It was far away, guttural and almost unintelligible, yet an unmistakable and very palpable malice crackled through the wires.

Instinct kicked in, and she pressed her ear closer to the phone, straining to make out the faint sounds. She heard muffled muttering, cursing and a high pitched sound that resembled a scream.

She shouted into the receiver, "Who is this? Who is there? Hello!"

There was nothing but silence once again before the voice came on, "Do you hear the voices as well? Do they haunt you at night?"

Instead of waiting for her to answer, the connection went dead. She switched on the bedside lamp with shaking

hands. Hopefully, the number would show on the caller ID.
It was no help. The only thing displayed was "Blocked". She
dialed *69 hoping she could get whoever called to pick up
once again. She felt utterly defeated when the recording
came on to state that the callback service was unavailable
for this number.

As she stared at the phone, another image appeared in her
mind. Another woman's life was about to be cut short.

She wished Mike was home. He and Guy were on a
stakeout tonight. There had been a rash of grave robberies
and they had to make sure nothing supernatural was
involved. Hutch would rather be on a stakeout than home
by herself.

Unable to sleep anymore, she walked into the kitchen. As
the water in the coffee pot heated up, she stared out the
kitchen window. The air around her vibrated with an
energy that seemed to always be present when a vision was
near.

Panic swept through her and raced like ice water through
her veins. There was nowhere to run, no place to hide. He
was on her in an instant. She felt the knife as it pierced the
hollow in her neck. Warm blood oozed from the wound.
The knife went in deeper. She could not scream.

She looked up through dead eyes to see the killer's face as it
contorted in a grotesque mask of rage. The hatred he felt
for her emitted from his very being. A gurgling sound
emitted from the wound in her throat. The light around her
faded away. Darkness surrounded her, closing in. She felt it
pressing against her, making it hard to breath.

There was a whooshing noise, and she found herself deep in the swamp. Voices surrounded her, all talking at once. She couldn't make out what they said. It was a cacophony of whispers. Then the vision left her. She was back in her kitchen, staring into the night. She looked over at the clock to find that it was now four thirty in the morning.

The air turned frigid, causing her to shiver. She walked into the living room and grabbed a blanket off the couch. She wrapped it around her, hoping to take away the chill.

This vision had such intensity that it was terrifying and with the phone call she'd just received, she found it hard to stop the shivering. She took a deep breath, trying to calm her racing heart.

Hutch gave up on going back to bed. She showered and decided to go into work early. Walking to her car, she thought she saw a movement near her car. She stopped and looked around, but the parking lot was empty.

Still, she had a strange sensation that someone was watching her. The hairs on the back of her neck stood up as a warning. As she walked to her car, her hand rested on the gun holstered at her side.

It was more than likely a junkie hoping to find a car unlocked so he could sleep it off; better yet, he may be in search of a few dollars for a fix. She listened for the sound of footsteps, but the area was eerily quiet this morning. The only thing she heard was her own breathing. As she went to unlock her car, she half expected to find someone waiting for her, but there was no one.

She looked under her car to make sure no one was lurking about. Before opening her car, she peered into the back-seat just in case. She didn't normally spook this easy, but hell, after the phone call and vision, it was easy to become frightened.

As she went to start her car, a shadow appeared next to the driver's side window.   She could have rolled down the window and touched it if she wanted to. Her heart pounded as she waited to see what the dark shadow would do. Goose bumps covered her whole body as she waited in anticipation of what was about to happen.

Whatever this dark shadow in front of her was, it certainly was not friendly. It was dark and sinister. She felt the evil that lived in it. Hutch did not want it to reach into the car and touch her, so she drove away, spinning out in the process.

Hutch had just made it to the police station when her phone rang, "Hutcherson."

The dispatcher exclaimed, "Detective Ledet asked that I call you. There has been another murder."

Hutch wrote down the pertinent information and headed out once more. She saw the reflection of the flashing lights come from the other side of the road and did a sharp u turn. She pulled in right behind Ledet's car.

A young beat cop came over to the car, "You Detective Hutcherson?"

"Yep."

"Detective Ledet said for you to do what you need to do. He is over by the water when you are ready."

Hutch asked, "What do we have?"

"A fisherman called in a dead woman over by the boat landing. There was a lot of mutilation done to her face."

Hutch thought the young cop would lose last night's supper right there. This must be his first homicide to work.

Instead of heading to where the body was, Hutch walked the perimeter of the crime scene before moving in.

After getting a sense of the crime scene, she moved to where the body was located. She knew what she would find - a body caught in gnarled limbs at the edge of the bayou. Her long brown hair flowed in the murky ripples of the water. Her body looked peaceful there, but Hutch knew that was a deception.

Regret filled her every pore. This was the young woman she had just dreamed of. Ledet informed her, "We will have to wait for her prints to be run through the system. There is no sign of a purse."

Hutch nodded her head in acknowledgment, "Someone will be missing her soon if they aren't already."

Hutch crouched down to look at the body. Even though she had been in the water for a while, she still appeared to be posed. Without thinking, she informed Ledet, "The killer called me right before he did this."

"Are you sure? How did he get your number? More importantly, how did he know to contact you? It's not like you have been in the news regarding this case."

Hutch informed him, "I believe he can talk to the dead as well. He may be an empath. I swore during a vision he looked right at me."

Ledet replied, "I don't like that at all. You fit the description of the women he is killing. What if he becomes fixated on you?"

Hutch patted her gun, "I will be ready for him if he does come after me."

"Yeah, I am sure you will. There is no guarantee that you will have time to protect yourself. These women were killed in a matter of seconds; you said so yourself."

Once back to the police station, Hutch looked through the missing persons' reports. She was so engrossed in her work, she never heard Mike walk up to her desk.

***

Mike watched the very attractive woman while she worked. Her eyes danced over the pages as her long, slender fingers gently swept the page. Her hair was unkempt from the long hours of tedious work. A few wisps fell in a cascading wave against her rosy cheeks. Instinctively, she reached up and pushed her hair behind her ear. His gaze moved to her lips. He loved those lips.

He couldn't help but take in her figure. She had the perfect hourglass shape. Her voluptuous breasts, curvy waist and full, round hips turned him on. She was exquisite under her professional looking shirt and pants. It excited him knowing that he was the only one in the precinct who knew what she looked like under her clothes. He thought about what he wanted to do to her when they got back home. Just the thought caused him to shift his stance as he felt a tightening in his groin.

She looked up to see him watching her and let out a sigh, "I don't think we will find out who she is tonight."

He held out his hand, "Let's go home. You look beat and need some rest."

***

As soon as they walked through her door, he pulled her into his arms. His long arms wrapped around her waist as her arms wrapped around his neck. Their bodies pressed against each other so closely that Hutch felt his heart beating in his chest. She closed her eyes and reveled in his intoxicating scent.

His body was hard and muscular. She felt his strength. "Can you hold me like this forever?"

He tipped her head up and kissed her before whispering in her ear, "Yes." His fingertips moved down her body, gliding across her back. Hutch shivered at his touch.

Hutch looked up at Mike and saw the passion in his eyes. She entwined her fingers in his hair and brought his lips to hers. The kiss was filled with raw passion. Mike held her even tighter. His tongue teased and tasted her as their hearts raced. His body was taut with desire. In one swift movement, Mike scooped her up and brought her to the bedroom.

Chapter 36

Hutch was almost asleep when the air in the room turned frigid. The air pulsated with evil. A dark shadow moved towards the bed. She blinked her eyes several times hoping her eyes were playing tricks on her. As it came closer to her, she froze in fear. The malevolence that surrounded her was terrifying. Her heart pounded so hard in her chest it actually hurt. Adrenaline raced through her veins. Her body shook.

The shadow hovered at the foot of the bed waiting for her to make the first move. All she could do was watch it. She was too scared to even reach out to wake Mike.

In the next instant, the shadow moved toward Mike. She feared it meant to harm Mike so she moved quickly and put her hands out in a manner to stop it, as if she could actually stop it physically.

She yelled out, "You are not welcome here. I order you to leave this place at once."

The black shadow moved away and then suddenly, it grew larger and became a solid black. As if a large gust of wind had blown through the bedroom, the covers and everything on the night stand went crashing to the floor. When Mike woke, the shadow disappeared. "What the hell happened?"

Hutch shook her head, "I'm not even sure. Something blew in all of a sudden."

As he reached out for her, he exclaimed, "You are as cold as ice."

Instead of responding, she just sank into his warm embrace. She let his warmth soak into her very being until she stopped trembling. He wrapped his arms around her tighter, bringing her back against his chest. For the first time since this started, she was afraid for the both of them.

***

Mike and Hutch stopped by the coffee shop before heading to work. Steam rose from the cup as she lifted it to her mouth to take a sip. An all too familiar chill ran through her.

Hutch did not want to have the vision in here with so many witnesses. She told Mike that she would wait for him in the car. She cradled the cup with both hands and hurried to the car, hoping to make it there before the mist consumed her vision. By the time she made it to the car, her world had gone silent as the mist became a dense fog. In the next instant, her world went dark. A numbing cold filled the car until there was no sign of warmth around her. Through the darkness, a light took shape. It wasn't long before the images appeared. Hutch tried to peer into the darkness to make out the images.

The images sharpened. A man walked to the bayou with a woman thrown over his shoulder. She felt the rage that emitted from him. A breeze rustled through the leaves on the trees as he made his way deeper. The ghosts of the ones he'd killed began to appear. Hutch couldn't make out what they were saying.

Once again, she attempted to make out his face. He was merely a black shadow. Even from this distance, she felt the evil that surrounded him. Suddenly, the images faded away. She was transported to a small room, a closet of some sort.

As she dropped the coffee from her grasp, she never even felt the hot liquid as it splashed on her lap. Once again, she looked through the eyes of the killer. She watched in horror as he took out tiny jars filled with liquid and placed them on a shelf. There were several tiny jars with the eyes and tongues of each victim he'd killed. He had caressed each jar lovingly before he locked the closet. As he passed by a mirror, he stopped to look at his reflection. The mirror was shattered, distorting his image. Disappointment filled her as once again she could not see his face. As he walked around the house, she searched for anything that would give her a clue as to his identity. Nothing so far could help her. Sensing that she was in his mind, the door slammed closed. The connection had broken before she found any relevant information.

Mike opening the car door sounded far away instead of right next to her. She looked at him with tears in her eyes, shaking uncontrollably. "It happened again. I saw through his eyes, but I couldn't get an image of his face."

Mike could tell that the vision had left her weak. He noticed the spilled coffee. "Did you burn yourself?"

Hutch looked down and grimaced at the spilled coffee, "Oh Mike, I am so sorry. I should have put the coffee down when I got into the car. All I thought about was getting to the safety of the car before the vision hit."

"I'm worried about you having scalded yourself and not the car. The coffee will clean up. Let's get you back home and make sure you didn't burn your legs."

As Mike started the car, Hutch blotted up the coffee as best as she could. Mike asked, "Did you make out anything useful?"

Hutch shook her head, "No, not really. I don't know if it was a new murder or something from the past. He keeps the eyes and tongues as trophies. He had them locked in some kind of closet. There was so much rage around him that all I could see was darkness surrounding him."

"Did the crime scene look familiar or maybe the house?"

"I'm not sure about the crime scene, but the house looked like an older house. When he passed by a mirror, I noticed it was shattered. His image was too distorted to make out."

Mike pondered what she'd said, "I wonder why the mirror was shattered? Maybe he isn't happy with his image."

The mirror being shattered had to be something significant, but what? He had such rage for these women. Did these women remind him of someone who'd hurt him?

Hutch continued to go over the details of her latest vision in her mind. She watched as the man put his hand up to the woman's neck with the knife. There, there it was. He had a tattoo on his wrist. How did she miss that before? She closed her eyes tighter and focused in on the tattoo. She called out for Mike, "Give me a piece of paper please. I need to draw a picture of this tattoo while I can still remember it."

Mike rushed to get a piece of paper and pencil. He did not want to disturb her any more than needed so he placed the pad and pencil in her hand. Without opening her eyes, she began to draw rapidly. She said out loud, "It was a snake of some kind on the inside of his wrist. I don't know how I missed it in the past. For a cab driver, his clothes were extremely neat looking. He dresses in black. I couldn't make out his hair color or style, they were still too distorted."

Hutch was exhausted from just reliving the vision. Her thoughts were too random and disjointed to do any good. Her head hurt so bad that her vision blurred.

Chapter 37

Ledet heard the buzz of his alarm clock and wanted to hit the snooze button just once. He didn't though. He forced himself to get out of bed. It was five a.m. and he wanted to get a run in before the heat and humidity were too bad. Perhaps the run would help him clear his mind. Was he so focused on this case that he had missed something relevant?

As he stumbled into the bathroom, he caught a glimpse of his image in the mirror. He hadn't realized how much this case had aged him. He would be thirty-five this year. It wouldn't be long before he was forty and until now, it never bothered him.

Looking closer at his image in the mirror, he noticed a few more gray hairs that weren't there a few months ago. He had always kept his hair short but not overly so. Perhaps a short crop style would hide the gray. Chuckling, he still remembered telling the barber in boot camp, "just a little off the top." He never expected to see all of his hair fall to the floor. Every young man in the barber shop walked out rubbing their newly bald head.

The beginnings of crow's feet started to appear around his eyes. Men are supposed to age gracefully, but he, on the other hand, was not ready to age.

As soon as he stepped outside for his run, the mugginess of the morning hit him flat in the face. It was going to be a hot day. He was ready for winter. He put his earphones in and turned on his MP3 player. If he was lucky, the music would keep his mind off of the case for a while. He needed something other than dead bodies to keep his mind occupied. Maybe he should start dating. It had been a while since his last failed relationship.

The run helped him wake up. By the time he made it back home, he was drenched in sweat. He jumped in a warm shower before getting ready for work. While in the shower, he lathered his face and shaved away the stubble. He had been considering growing a goatee. The way this case occupied his every waking moment, this would be the perfect time.

After dressing, he stepped into the kitchen to grab a quick bite to eat. At least he remembered to set the coffee pot before his run. He couldn't start his morning off without coffee. As he headed out the door his phone rang. "Ledet."

"Detective, you have another victim."

After getting all the pertinent details, he responded, "I'm on my way. Have you called Bryant yet?"

The dispatcher responded, "I tried, but didn't get an answer. I will try again after I hang up with you."

"Just tell him to meet me there."

As soon as Ledet got in his car, his phone rang again. It was Bryant calling, "Sorry about that. I didn't hear my phone ringing. I'm on my way mon ami."

"Why don't you stop and pick up the coffee? Something tells me we will need it."

"Mais oui. See you there, mon ami."

***

Bryant headed over to Café Orleans to get their coffee before going to the crime scene. The aroma of warm beignets and freshly brewed coffee filled his senses. This place was extremely busy. The hum of customers drowned out the sounds of the espresso machines in use. Unable to resist the tempting smell of the beignets, he picked him and his partner up a few.

Downtown traffic was a bitch, and it took him longer than he expected. By the time Bryant made it out to the crime scene, the coffee was lukewarm.

When he arrived, Ledet, Hutch, and Dr. Ortego were already at the crime scene. He handed out the coffee as he looked over at Detective Hutcherson, hiding his contempt for her joining the team. He would prefer not to have her working with them, but hid his disapproval.

Ledet stared down at the young woman. "I don't think she even knew what was happening."

Bryant approached him, "The perp didn't leave us any trace evidence."

Ledet grunted in acknowledgement as he inspected the crime scene. Once again, the killer was meticulous about leaving no evidence. He also did a good job of making it impossible for the detectives to do their jobs. Hopefully, forensics would find more evidence, but he had a gut feeling that wouldn't happen.

Ledet listened as Dr. Ortego went into the details of the victim's death, "Time of death occurred around three a.m. this morning. As with the previous victims, exsanguination was the cause of death. I will run toxicology reports just to make sure we don't miss anything. When I examined the body, I didn't notice any other signs of injury. I will know more when I get her on the table and can do a more thorough job."

***

As he spoke, Ledet took notes in his tablet and started working on his report. Technology was great when it came to note taking. He no longer went back to the office to write a report. Now, he just synced his tablet with his computer and he had everything needed for his report at his fingertips. Ledet knew some cops still preferred their pen and paper, but in his opinion the less time he spent writing reports meant more time to catch criminals.

Ledet had Hutch walking the scene, but he also wanted to absorb the crime scene. Each crime scene had a story to tell, but you had to be patient and let the story unfold before your eyes. He wanted to compare notes and see how their notes differed.

One of the forensic techs came over to Ledet, "Detective, we are finishing up here."

Ledet instructed him, "Send me the report as soon as you can."

"Yes, sir."

Detective Bryant went through what little of the victim's personal belongings were at the scene, "As usual, there isn't much here."

"Damn."

Bryant asked, "Do you think we have enough for a profile?"

"Mais non, not yet. He just isn't giving us enough."

Ledet surveyed the crime scene one more time. If his suspicions were correct, this killer had no intentions of stopping. Forensics finished up, and the medical examiner's office prepared to move the body. The killer would not stop until they stopped him.

Once back at the office, Ledet planned to run the victimology through ViCAP again. He would continue his search for any similar matches to the M.O.

***

As Hutch looked at the young crime scene tech taking photos, a chill ran through her body, cutting her to the bone. There was a flicker of something cold in his eyes. If she had not known better, she would have sworn something evil lurked behind his eyes. A tremor snaked down her spine at that thought.

Hutch couldn't shake the feeling that the killer was watching the scene. She instructed the crime scene photographer, "Get photos of the crime scene from all angles, please. I want to ensure we don't miss anything and also, take photos of the crowd."

"Yes, ma'am."

Chapter 38

In her dream, Hutch once again found herself looking through the murderer's eyes. She watched in horror as he grabbed the woman from the shadows of the alley. The woman never had a chance to scream as the knife cut deep into her throat. Hutch felt helpless as the woman died. She tried to call out for someone to help but couldn't.

Next, she was transported to the marshland. She pushed her way through the dense foliage. Fragments of moonlight penetrated the greenery. He continued moving closer to the bayou.

It was so real that Hutch swore she was there with him. She heard the crickets, felt the coolness of the air on her skin and smelled the damp scent of the earth. Breaking through the underbrush, he made his way to a clearing that led him to the bayou. The scene here was peaceful and serene, but that peacefulness would soon be shattered.

He turned his head slightly and breathed in the scent that came from the woman's hair. It reminded him of candy apples. The coppery scent of blood mixing with her scent gave him a rush like none other.

He dropped the body unmercifully to the ground. Her face, smeared with blood and dirt, was frozen in a mask of terror. A sound in the woods caught his attention. The ghosts of those he'd killed emerged from the woods. Rage built in him as their voices echoed in his head.

He posed her in the murky water of the bayou. He stood at the precipice of the bayou looking down at her. A satisfied smile teased the corner of his mouth.

Hutch bolted upright in bed. If only she could erase the images from her mind. Every time she smiled, she envisioned the wicked grin of the killer. Hutch must stop this murderer. She had to help these poor women find peace.

Chapter 39

Mike and Hutch were walking into the restaurant when her phone rang. *Crap, dispatch again. So much for a quiet evening with Mike.* She would have to let him know he wouldn't be having that quiet evening, after all, "Hutch."

"Ma'am, I hate to ruin your evening, but we've got another dead body. Detectives Ledet and Bryant are on their way."

She jotted down the particulars from the dispatcher and replied "I'm not too far away. I'll be there in a few."

Mike waved at the maître d' as they headed out. It would be a quick drive thru before going to the crime scene.

A haze of activity confirmed that they had arrived at the crime scene. Half a dozen cop cars lined the streets and the ambulance to carry the body away. Blue and red flashing lights lit up the night sky. People started to mill around, curious about what happened. Forms shifted through the lights before merging with the darkness once again.

Hutch stood in front of the car and surveyed the crime scene. It bothered her that anyone was capable of doing such things to another human. With everything that she'd recently witnessed, she should not be surprised at the amount of pain another individual was capable of inflicting upon someone, but it did bother her.

Before entering the crime scene, she closed her eyes to erase the images of the previous crime scenes from her mind. She wanted to look at the scene with fresh eyes. Perhaps this time she would see their killer.

Steady now, images and emotions gone, she sought out Ledet. Forensic technicians were busy collecting evidence and processing the scene. She didn't need to examine any evidence. There wouldn't be enough to bother with, but they would attempt to collect what they could. She tried not to focus on anything but the overall energy left after a murder. She needed to listen carefully to what the victim's tortured soul tried to tell her. It was as if she felt the rage the killer had for the victim.

Ledet stood near the coroner's van wearing dark blue jeans and a white cotton shirt. He was a handsome man standing six-two with massive shoulders and a well-defined chest. His biceps struggled to stay contained in his shirt. At first glance, he appeared rough with a cold square jaw chiseled out of stone. However, as she got to know him, he was nothing more than a gentle giant.

She watched as a range of emotions danced across his face. She saw sadness, contempt, anger, and sympathy. For a moment, she thought she felt a rush of fear course through his body. Could they be afraid of the same thing, that they wouldn't be able to stop this killer?

She watched as the media vans arrived. As soon as they finished setting up, they would broadcast continuously in every format at their disposal about the body being found. Soon, they would cast stones and make accusations about the inability of the New Orleans Police Department to stop this monster. There would be a public outcry for this monster to be stopped at all cost.

This case haunted their every waking moment and exhausted the department's manpower. Several news media outlets had already criticized the department openly for not having brought in the FBI and creating a specialized task force. They hadn't been privy to the actual workings of the case, and Hutch prayed that it stayed that way. If the state, or even the feds became involved, it would only complicate things.

Chapter 40

The vision came without warning, right before her open eyes. She found herself deep in the swampland at night; the land illuminated by the moonlight that filtered through the dense canopy of branches. Hutch was drawn deeper into the swampland as if by a magical force or beacon of some kind. She made her way through the dense underbrush.   Apprehension and dread filled her as she moved further into the area.

Up ahead, the underbrush thinned. As she drew closer, she heard the water as it broke against the bank of the bayou. Her heart pounded in her chest as she made her way to the clearing.

Hutch knew what horror she was about to see. There would be a lifeless body waiting to be discovered. As she looked into the murky water, she saw the still body of the young woman. Her hair splayed out around her head, shimmering in the moonlight. She looked so peaceful lying in the water, almost as if she was asleep. Her face held the pallor of death. Her eyelids were closed, hiding the fact that the killer had removed her eyes. The water washed away the blood that once streaked across her face. The gaping wound in her throat caught her attention. A dark, vicious liquid oozed from her wound as the last of her life's essence made its way into the murky water surrounding her.

Hutch's nerves tingled with fear as she looked around to see if the killer still lurked about. She sensed the presence of evil nearby. Somewhere nearby a small, almost imperceptible sound caught her attention. Fear had her frozen in place as she looked over to where the sound came from. Suddenly, a blood soaked hand reached out from the dense swampland and grabbed her arm, dragging her into the woods. She tried to free herself as she told herself that this was merely a dream, a nightmare actually. This wasn't possible; this was just a vision. The hand gripping her shoulder still felt real as it continued to shake her.

She almost passed out when the monster whispered in her ear, "Grace."

It took sheer willpower to look over at the face of the man leaning in to whisper in her ear. Her heart raced in her chest. Nothing was there except a black shadow. From behind her, she heard the distinct noise of a knife being removed from its protective sheath. This couldn't be happening. It was only a vision. Her eyes darted to the left to see the moonlight glint off the blade of the knife. Blood from the recent kill dripped off of the tip. The shadow standing next to her was dark and menacing. Her heartbeat pounded in her ears.

She squeezed her eyes shut, not wanting to see anymore and surely not wanting to feel the knife on her delicate flesh.

She shouted out, "Enough, I can't witness anymore right now." Abruptly the vision dissipated. She waited for the killer's grip on her shoulder to leave her, but instead, it only strengthened. She struggled to free herself from his grasp. It just wasn't possible. What was going on? Why did she still feel the killer's grip on her shoulder?

The killer shook her once more and called out, "Grace, are you okay? Please open your eyes. Talk to me."

In that instant, Hutch recognized Mike's voice. "Grace, please open your eyes."

Mike watched as Hutch's eyes fluttered open. As Hutch looked around, an intense foreboding gripped her body. Who was this monster? She prayed that no one else had been murdered.

It took several hours for her to feel like herself. Mike hovered over her until her pallor returned to normal. She felt drained and nauseous for most of the day.

She relied on coffee to help her get through the rest of the day. As soon as she entered the break room, the sugary scent of hot doughnuts greeted her. She took one out and bit into the warm fluffy pastry. The greasy sweetness instantly filled her mouth. It was like biting into a heavenly pillow of doughnut goodness. They were as soft as cotton and as light as air. Each bite melted in her mouth as it tantalized her taste buds. She let out a moan of pleasure as she savored another bite. After taking a sip of coffee, she licked the sugar from her fingers. Before returning to her desk, she grabbed a second doughnut. This was what she needed to get through the day. As she bit into her second doughnut, she pondered how something so good was supposed to be so bad for you.

As she finished her coffee, her phone rang, "Detective Hutcherson another body has been found." Ice ran through her veins. She shivered involuntarily as she wrote down the information.

The vision was pulled from her memory as she headed out. Once again, it was out in the open, fresh and new. Before even arriving at the scene, she knew it would be a female with a bloody gash on her throat.

The air at the crime scene was charged with electrical energy. The hair on the back of her neck and arms stood at attention. All around her, voices began to speak at once. A cacophony of emotions washed over her – pain, suffering, hopelessness, rage and a desperate sadness she could barely contain. She became bombarded with too much all at once. Through all of this mental chaos, one voice intensified, "You must help us. Please help us find peace. You must stop him."

She wanted to help them, but how? Her vision of the killer was nothing more than a black blur. He left no trace evidence for them to explore. Something had to give and give soon.

Her mind spun out of control. Voices and emotions churned in her head. Horrible eyeless faces flashed before her eyes. They called out to her, begging for help.

Tears streamed down her face as she tried to silence them so that she could get a feel for the crime scene. A voice in the distance called out to her, "Hutch, are you okay?"

The voices of the dead faded away. Detective Ledet asked her once more, "Are you okay?"

She wasn't comfortable telling him about the rush of emotions and voices calling out to her. She just nodded her head as she wiped the tears from her eyes. "I am fine.

There is no reason to worry. Sometimes the energy level is high at a crime scene is all."

Chapter 41

Ledet sat at his desk and looked at the pile of case folders in front of him. He really should catch up on his active cases while they waited for some developing evidence to help locate the serial killer lurking about the streets of New Orleans. He grabbed the top folder, laying it open amongst the clutter on his desk and flipped it open. Needing to refresh his memory, he read the first few pages before his mind drifted back to the current serial killer case.

He felt sorry for Hutch. It must be hard to watch someone being killed and be unable to prevent it. As cops, they were trained to react yet her hands were tied so to speak. She watched it happen as if she was right there, but it was only a vision. She couldn't literally reach out and touch the man. Ledet wanted to get ahead of this killer and stop him before he murdered again.

He closed the file he was trying to catch up on and let out a deep sigh. No matter how hard he tried to occupy his mind on other trivial matters, he kept circling back to these murders.

He was missing something, but damn, he couldn't figure out what. All they had was what Hutch saw, which unfortunately wasn't much. Hell, until recently, Ledet never gave much thought to the supernatural or paranormal. However, with the last few cases they'd had here in New Orleans, he had learned to keep his mind open to all possibilities.

Somehow they had to use what information they had to come up with a profile of the killer. The crime scenes revealed nothing forensically essential. The killer wore gloves. No fingerprints were found on the body or at the scene. There were tire tracks, but that hadn't gotten them anywhere. Over half the tires sold in New Orleans matched that particular model of tire. They had nothing to go on, no leads, and no evidence. The only thing they knew with certainty was the same person committed these murders.

He had more people breathing down his neck than he liked. Everyone wanted to know why they hadn't stopped this killer and how many young women would be murdered before they captured this guy.

Chapter 42

Hutch opened her closet and looked over the clothes, trying to decide what to wear today. She needed to feel a little more human today, so she chose a simple black skirt that hit right above her knee and a lovely royal blue silk shirt. For a change, she felt motivated to get the day started.

She walked into the kitchen to find Mike busy cooking. He looked completely irresistible as he cooked. The wonderful aroma of bacon, eggs and coffee greeted her. Her stomach grumbled, reminding her that she'd missed supper last night.

He did not notice her until he turned around from the kitchen sink. When he saw her, he gave her a huge grin; it made her knees buckle. He was the only man able to turn her insides to jello with just a simple look.

He walked over and gave her a kiss, "Good morning."

She pulled him in closer and kissed him back, "Good morning to you too."

He looked her up and down, "You look gorgeous this morning."

She ran her hands over his bare chest, "You look handsome as well."

"I wanted to do something nice for you this morning, so I made us a good breakfast. You seemed to be sleeping well for a change and I didn't have the heart to wake you."

"You are too good to me."

He grinned. "Now, sit down while I prepare us something to eat."

"You don't need any help?"

He swatted at her behind as he eased her to the barstool, "Sit."

While he busied himself, she sat back and watched. She took in his well-defined muscles and washboard stomach. As he moved, his muscles rippled. He wore loose fitting pants, but she could just imagine the well sculpted muscles of his legs. His hair was still tousled. His jaw was square; his cheekbones were chiseled, and he had the most mesmerizing brown eyes that you could get lost in.

Everything tasted as wonderful as it smelled. "This is wonderful." She walked over to him, "I love you Mike."

He wrapped his arms around her and brought her closer to him, "I love you with all my heart." She kissed him deeply.

"I don't know what I would do without you in my life. You have been through a lot with me. It scares the hell out of me that my dreams are becoming more vivid."

"You know I am here for you. I will be here no matter what."

Just talking with Mike helped abate some of her fears. The storm was just beginning though, and the worst was yet to come.

On the way to work, Hutch stopped by a local voodoo shop to learn about charms and keeping the evil spirits away. She hoped to find something to ward off the malevolent force that surrounded the killer's image in her visions and allow her to see his face. At this point, she was willing to try anything.

As she walked into the store, the bell above the door dinged. She'd met Paul Decimus when they stopped Bianca Honore from unleashing her army of zombies on New Orleans.

He walked over and gripped her hand in a firm shake, "How is the new gift coming along, cher?"

She shook her head, "I still don't know if I would call it a gift."

"Oh cher, you shouldn't consider it a curse. Once you learn how to control your abilities, you will come to appreciate your gift. You are one of the lucky ones who sees that this world is populated by more than just flesh and blood beings."

"I wish I understood why my gift has suddenly matured into something more."

Paul Decimus replied, "I see that Rayne is still watching over you."

Hutch nodded her head in agreement, "She is."

"She is worried about you. Why don't you tell me what you have been experiencing so that I may assist you?"

Hutch recounted the psychic experiences over the last few months, and Paul responded, "That is interesting. So these ghosts are now not only seeking you out, but you are seeing the killings through the killer's eyes."

"These women are begging me for help. If I could get rid of the black shadow that surrounds the killer, I may be able to see his face."

"You have come to the right place. I will help you control your abilities so that you can stop this monster. I will also help you understand your gifts. It looks as if you have been given a specific purpose to help these women. You must keep your mind open and follow your intuition. You HAVE been given a very special gift. Not too many people have out of body experiences. There are only a few individuals who are extra sensitive and can leave their body to go where the actual vision takes place."

She let out a sigh, "I think he has seen me."

Paul cringed, "This man is very dangerous. We must protect you from him. Let's make you a special Gris Gris and I will also put a charm in it to help you see his image. We must find out who he is. I wish I could be with you at all times, but maybe we can get Rayne to help us."

Hutch shook her head, "Rayne sees him exactly as I do. She suggested I come to you for help. I suspect even the victims see him as I do, merely a black shadow."

Paul considered everything she said, "There is a chance that Rayne helped supercharge your abilities. That could explain why you see through the killer's eyes and the victims' eyes."

"If having these visions would help solve this case, I would be more than happy to be the vessel for them. But so far, all I have seen were gruesome murders that don't bring us any closer to stopping this killer."

Paul reminded her, "Just remember, above all else, it is most important to keep your psychic world open. When the visions start, you must remember to concentrate on how much you want to stop him. Think of the women who need your help- dead and alive. This will help clear your mind. Above all else, you must focus on him. Give me your hands. Let's do a little experiment."

Hutch handed him her hands, "Close your eyes and focus on one of your visions."

As soon as she closed her eyes, images flashed before her eyes. They moved too fast for her to get a clear picture and then as if someone hit the pause button, they froze. She felt herself being transported to a front porch of an old worn down house. The vision was so real that she could smell the damp earth and decaying leaves. The flower beds out front were taken over by ivy and the honeysuckle grew rampant, traveling up the columns of the house. Someone had neglected the yard for years. She swallowed back her fear and concentrated on everything she saw. She feared another dead woman was here. She slowly made her way into the house. Dust and cobwebs covered everything. When she saw the broken mirror, her skin instantly began to crawl. Evil dwelled here; this was the killer's house. Fear clung to her like a second skin, but she pushed on. She felt as if she was walking through an ethereal hell.

Before moving deeper into the house, she stopped to listen. She heard someone humming. Her mind screamed for her to wake up from this vision, but she must keep going if she wanted to stop this killer. She moved closer to where the noise came from. She slipped into the small room to find a bare chested man sitting at a desk. Something deep inside of her told her he was naked. He sat with his back turned to her, staring into a closet. She didn't want to look in that closet. She knew what was in there. She saw it in her visions before; it was the small glass containers that held the eyes and tongues of his victims.

As he picked up a jar, the room was suddenly filled with the sound of his bizarre laughter. Goosebumps crept up Hutch's body as her uneasiness increased. As glasses clinked together, Hutch moved closer to see what he was doing. He picked up another jar and lovingly rubbed it against his cheek before putting it back.

She needed to see how many jars were in there. This could be the only way they had of knowing how many women he'd killed to date. This was the purpose of this vision. Maybe she would finally get a good look at his face. She moved even closer, until she was peering over his shoulder. Suddenly, the laughter became almost hysterical. He wore nothing but a white mask on his face. Only his eyes were visible. He stared deep into her eyes. His eyes were cold, dark, empty and dead. His laughter turned demented. Without warning, the laughter stopped and he whispered softly, "You can't see me, but I see you Detective Grace Hutcherson." He picked up a jar for her to look in. It contained the eyes belonging to one of the victims.

Her mind reeled from the fact that he not only called her by her name but that he acknowledged he saw her. It was as if he knew she would be coming. Her body shook violently with that realization.

Suddenly, her mind was filled with darkness, but a calming darkness. She heard Paul calling out to her, "It is okay Grace. You are in my shop. Take some deep breaths."

The reality of the dream had her shaking. The murderer knew she would have this vision, but how? He'd prepared for this very vision by wearing a mask. Anger exploded deep inside of her with such ferocity that it startled her for a moment. It surged through her body, seeped into her pores and filled her mouth with the bitter taste of bile. She didn't turn away from the feeling; she instead savored it and let it strengthen her.

Instead of speaking, Paul just watched her as her mind churned with a multitude of thoughts and emotions. She let out an exasperated sigh, "What good is this 'gift' as you call it if I can't keep him from killing these women? We can say in the end that I am giving them closure, but honestly how does that help? They are still dead, and their loved ones have to go on without them. I can't bring them back, no one can."

"Cher, you must understand that you have no control over fate, destiny or whatever you choose to call it. That is not what this gift is meant for. You are not expected to intervene or even right all wrongs. You have been given a gift to help these girls find peace from their violent deaths. Cher, you are a very empathic person. It is in your nature to help others, and this may come to include sharing in their pain and suffering. You are developing the ability to feel every experience of not only the victims, but also the killer." He grasped Hutch's hands tight, "Cher, there is another possibility of why you see the visions so clearly; this killer may be someone you know or run into often."

Fear snaked down her spine at that very possibility. Was that why she couldn't make out his face?

He saw the disbelief on her face, "Cher, it's only a possibility, but it concerns me that you saw through his eyes and felt what the victims feel. Maybe your gift is progressing, but we also need to consider that you know the killer."

Hutch's stomach clenched as she listened to what he had to say. Her whole body shook at the possibility. Paul reached into his pocket, "I made this just in case, but you definitely need this now."

She looked at the bracelet Paul handed her. It was a gorgeous black beaded bracelet. He informed her, "It is made of hematite. You must wear this all the time. This will keep you protected and keep the negative energies at bay."

As she put on the bracelet, she asked, "Will I still be able to see the visions?"

"You should still see the visions, but it should prevent him from intruding on your mind. He seems to be more powerful than I initially realized."

***

He craved his time in his private sanctuary with his mementos. It was his special time. This was where he could be alone with his trophies.

This was where he found true fulfillment from each kill. In here, there was nothing but him and his memories. It was his personal paradise. Being here rejuvenated him, renewed his focus, gave him strength and now he chose to share it with Detective Hutcherson. How he wished he could see her face right now. What did she think after witnessing these treasures he held so dear?

Chapter 43

He watched and waited in the dark shadows. He waited another ten minutes after the car left the parking lot before making his move. As he slid the lock pick in the door, he waited anxiously to hear it click open. He quickly entered her home and shut the door.

He stood in the silence, admiring her home. He took in the coziness of the small living space. The house was surprisingly neat and clean.

As he walked into the living room, he took in the sparse furnishings. There was a couch, two recliners, an entertainment center and a coffee table. The house was devoid of pictures and knickknacks. The two lovers still hadn't made the small apartment theirs yet. Perhaps they weren't sure about their living arrangements or were they too busy?

He moved further into the apartment. The kitchen was a small, cozy room. He noticed that the water was still warm in the coffee pot and searched through the cabinets for a coffee "k" cup and mug. Soon, the smell of coffee filled the kitchen. He breathed in the fragrant brew and took a tentative sip. This was better than the brand he bought. He made a mental note to pick some up at the store. After finishing his coffee, he rinsed the mug thoroughly and placed it back in the cabinet.

He walked into the bedroom to find the covers thrown back and unmade. They must have been in a hurry to leave this morning or could it be that she preferred not to bother with

such trivial matters as making a bed. He surveyed the room
and realized that here must be where the young lovers
spent most of their time. There was an understated
elegance to this room.

Wanting to feel close to her, he undressed, neatly folding
his clothes and placing them on the dresser. He carefully
arranged the bedcovers and slipped beneath the sheets.
They were cool and sensual against his bare skin. He buried
his head in her pillow, reveling in the smell of her. Her
scent was intoxicating. It reminded him of summer nights
heady with the scent of gardenias. He became aroused and
for a moment, he considered finding relief here in her bed.
Then he recalled his mother's words. Besides, he couldn't
leave any DNA evidence for her to find.

He got out of the bed and carefully remade it, placing the
note he wrote on her pillow. As he dressed, he perused the
dresser drawers. He opened the first drawer and
rummaged through it. Nothing there called out to him. The
second drawer proved to be more interesting. It contained
her unmentionables. He stopped to linger here, caressing
each of the sexy bikini panties and lacy bras.

He pulled a pair of black lace panties from the drawer, held
them up to his nose and inhaled deeply. His pulse
quickened as he thought of her sliding these up her long,
sexy legs. Before closing the drawer, he stuffed the black
lace panties in his pocket as a memento of being here. He
gave the room one final look before leaving the apartment.
If only he could be here when the sweet young Detective
Hutcherson arrived home tonight to discover the note he'd
left her.

***

As soon as she got home, Hutch walked into the living room and plopped down on a recliner, wrapping the afghan snugly around her shoulders. She couldn't remember the last time she'd felt this exhausted. It wasn't only physical exhaustion, but mental as well. As she laid back against the cool leather, a sense of foreboding came over her. The energy in the house was off. She looked around to see if perhaps there was a ghost.

She leaned back in the recliner once more trying to relax her frayed nerves. Her recent conversation with Paul Decimus played through her mind. Could she learn how to control her "gift"? Why were these ghosts seeking her out? Was this what fate had in store for her life?

She closed her eyes. If only she could get a few minutes of uninterrupted rest. Then she would feel better, and think clearer. Mike and Guy were bowling tonight, so she had a few hours to herself. As much as she loved Mike, they each needed their own time away from each other. They would drive each other crazy if they did not have that time. As it was, they rode to and from work together and worked cases together. They spent most of their time together.

Sleep came fast to her, as did the vision. Strobe light flashes of images ran through her mind. She tried to piece them together. The vision was reminiscent of an old silent movie playing in her head once again. She watched in horror as the black shadow opened a door and entered a house. Excitement pulsed through him as he entered the house. She waited to see the flash of a knife blade, but instead he just walked through the house. It took her a moment to realize that the house was hers. The killer was in her house!

She bolted awake, shattering the vision. She reached for her gun she'd placed on the end table and searched the house, armed and ready for the intruder. She checked behind the curtains and every corner of the house. The bedroom was the last room to check, she slowly opened the door. She stopped in her tracks when she saw the note on her pillow and that the bed was made.

Hutch played the morning back through her mind and didn't remember either of them taking the time to make the bed. Her heart raced as the vision played in her mind once more. The killer had been here. He had been in their bed! She knew without a doubt that the letter was for her.

She took her cell phone out of her pocket and called Mike. She hated that she was about to ruin his night, "The killer came to the house, laid in our bed, went through our things and even left me a note."

Rage built up in him instantly, "Get out of the house now. Guy and I will be there shortly."

"He is long gone now. I will have the crime scene techs give the house a once over. Maybe, we will get lucky, and he left us some fingerprints."

Mike replied, "Please, do me this favor and call from the car. Wait for them to go through the house. I want you out of that house while you are by yourself."

Hutch would be wasting her time arguing with Mike. He was treating her more like a scared woman rather than what she really was, a damn good police officer. Not wanting to hurt his ego, she complied with his wish. She refused to wait in the car while the crime scene techs went through her house though. She wanted to watch everything they did. She wanted to be the first to know if they found something.

It had taken almost ten minutes before the first responding officer arrived at her apartment. She met him by his car and explained what happened. She followed him through the apartment; making sure no one was there. He wanted to confirm it for himself before sending in the crime scene techs. Hutch understood protocol, but she was a fellow officer and knew how to secure the scene, after all. She let out an exasperated gasp after mumbling to herself, "Men."

Mike arrived at the same time as the crime scene techs. As he spoke to the crime scene techs, Hutch walked through the apartment being careful not to touch anything. She wanted to see every step he'd made through their tiny apartment. She watched in horror as he took a pair of panties out of the drawer before leaving.

She instructed one of the crime scene techs, "Make sure you dust the dresser for prints. He took something out of the second drawer."

"Yes, ma'am."

Unadulterated rage coursed through her body. He'd violated her home; her private domain. She focused on the anger, hoping it helped her focus in on his face.

She continued to nurture that hate and anger, letting it grow inside of her. She would not let him beat her. She couldn't fall apart now; so many women depended on her.

This was the quiet before the storm. He was becoming even more dangerous. He was insane. She took several deep breaths to calm her mind and steady her pounding heart. She must focus if she hoped to see his face.

Later that night, she and Mike checked into a hotel. After knowing he'd climbed naked into their bed, Hutch refused to sleep in that bed tonight. No, tomorrow she would go out and buy new sheets and burn those he'd laid on.

As she curled into Mike's warm embrace, she fell into an unsettled sleep. Her dreams were vivid and frightening.

The next morning Hutch went back to their tiny apartment to perform a cleansing. She stopped by Paul's shop to purchase some white candles before heading home. In each room of the apartment, she poured a circle of salt and lit the white candle in the center of the circle. She repeated the mantra Paul gave her in each room until she didn't feel the negative energy the killer left behind.

Chapter 44

Hutch and Mike had just placed their order at Beazell's On The Bayou when she felt a chill in the air. Sitting right next to Mike was Rayne Simoneaud. Hutch let out an inward groan. Her life went from visions, to an occasional ghost making an appearance, and now they regularly popped in on her. At least where Rayne sat it appeared she was talking to Mike and not to herself.

As Rayne looked over at the couple with the baby next to them, sorrow enveloped her. "I will never see my child born. Sometimes the grief is too much."

Hutch never stopped to consider the pain that kept Rayne trapped in this world. She couldn't imagine what the poor woman was going through - betrayed by her lover, the father of her child, killed before her child was born. That alone would be too much for Hutch to handle.

"I am so sorry Rayne. I never once stopped to imagine what you are going through."

"I thought when Dominic and Bianca were killed I could move on. Then I felt a malevolent force following you. I couldn't leave you to face that alone."

Hutch suspected more than that kept Rayne from moving on. Perhaps she could not move on because of her untimely death, never seeing her child born, but could it be that Rayne did sense a malevolent force lurking about? She had to solve this murder case so that perhaps it freed the victims and Rayne.

Forgetting that she was no longer mortal, Rayne reached out to her. "Grace you must listen to me, cher. This killer may have the same psychic abilities as you, especially since he can make this type of connection with you. I fear that I led him straight to you."

Hutch found herself startled by that realization. "I sure hope not. If this man does possess the same psychic powers as me then there is no telling what evil he is capable of performing. It can also mean he will always be one step ahead of us."

This man was pure evil. Hutch thought back to her vision and how he'd mumbled to himself while slashing at the sky. Did he see them taking form around him and attempted to get them to leave him alone? Was he trying to kill them again? He was so full of hate and rage.

Chapter 45

Maggie Jenkins slapped the snooze button on her alarm clock and pulled the blanket over her head. She refused to open her eyes. Just as she dozed off again, the alarm went off. She wanted to hit the snooze button. She and her friends had gone bar hopping until the wee hours of the morning. Even though she stayed out all night, she had limited herself to only one drink, which was more than she could say for her friends. They were probably still in bed and would be there most of the day.

She moaned as she rolled out of bed. Who'd ever heard of waking up at this ungodly hour on a Saturday morning, but if she wanted to win the race, she needed to get out there and train. Her competition would already be out on the bayou paddling away.

As she walked into the kitchen, she looked out the window and took in the beautiful sky as the coffee finished brewing. Bleary eyed, she took in the first streaks of pink that danced across the dark gray sky. She poured herself a cup of coffee and headed back to her room to dress before heading out. She pulled on her shorts, t-shirt, and running shoes. She grabbed the ponytail holder from her wrist and pulled her hair back before heading out. She made sure to grab herself a Greek yogurt to take with her before leaving the house. Eventually, she would need the calories and the protein to get her through the morning.

In no time, she had the kayak loaded, and left. For this race, she would be a one person team. She had been looking forward to this race since she saw the announcement in the paper a few months back. She found the small one person kayak in the want ads for next to nothing. After spending time to clean it up and make sure it didn't sink, she was ready to go. Each day she improved her time and if the current was right, she should have no problem making good time. Her friends teased her, saying she was crazy for wanting to compete with these guys. Especially since most of them had been racing for years now and were pros.

Maggie just shrugged her shoulders and let the words roll off her back. Everyone had to start off at the bottom. No one started off as a pro. Hell, she didn't even care if she won. She wanted to compete and finish the course.

At the boat landing, she stretched well before taking the kayak from the bed of her small pick-up truck. Maggie was so engrossed in what she was doing that she didn't pay attention to her surroundings. She never even heard the man as he came up behind her. It wasn't until he grabbed her from behind that she realized someone else was there.

***

He did not expect her to fight back. Although petite, she possessed a strength unmatched by any of the other women he had killed. She was quick and had the reflexes of a fighter. As he went to slit her throat, she bucked beneath him. She bared her nails and clawed at him. She attempted to throw him off, but he had a good foot over her and weighed almost one hundred pounds more than she did.

Before he knew what happened, she flipped him to the ground. He saw red from the rage that consumed him. The bitch would pay for doing this. He grabbed her ankles before she could get very far and pulled her down to the ground. She swatted at his face and screamed, "Get off of me. Someone please help."

Her nails made contact with his face and tore four neat gashes down his left cheek. She pummeled his body with her small fists, but her gestures only annoyed him and did nothing to deter him from his mission.

Even though she fought for her life, she was afraid. He felt it radiating helplessly from her very being. The smell of fear emitted from her body; a body that would soon cease to function. She knew he had the power to end her life. The fear he induced in her was orgasmic for him.

She continued her ear piercing screams that tortured his ears and brought on a splitting headache. The piercing screams did nothing except aggravate him further. He took the knife and began to viciously slash at her face instead of just slitting her throat and being done with it. She tried to fight off the blows. He moved from her face down to her breasts where he stabbed the knife deep into her body. Finally, he expertly slit her throat with a quick flick of his wrist. Her body shuddered underneath him as her blood flowed onto the ground.

It was as if something or someone else took control of his body. He continued long after she died to slash, jab and tear her flesh with the knife. He closed his eyes, and the features on his face contorted as rage, hatred and a sick pleasure overcame his body.

When finished, his shoulders ached as exhaustion moved through his body. His hand even cramped from where it had grasped the knife. He leaned forward and rested his head on hers as he breathed in heavily. If someone passed by them, it would appear as if two lovers were exhausted from a round of passionate lovemaking. As he looked down at the body, he was pleased to see that in his rage he had not cut her eyes. He carefully removed the eyes and tongue and put them in the little container he'd brought for this very purpose.

***

Hutch watched in horror as the blood from the latest victim filled her mind. She had been in a dead sleep when she felt herself being transported to another place. This time she looked through the victim's eyes instead of seeing the murder from the killer's eyes. Hutch felt each horrifying stab as he continued to stab the poor woman repeatedly. She almost passed out from the excruciating pain. For just a moment, she thought the killer had stopped. She looked down at the body and saw that it was her and not the victim before he continued with his madness. There was recognition in his eyes.

As the soul left the body, there was another whoosh. Hutch found herself in the killer's body. He scanned the area to make sure that no one was around. He stood up and looked at the blood splattered ground and the body before wiping the knife on his jeans and heading back to his car.

Hutch sat up in bed and shook Mike. With tears in her eyes, she told him, "He did it again. It was awful."

Mike rolled over in bed and partially sat up, "What did you say?"

"There's been another murder. He had so much rage. The attack was vicious. He took pleasure in mutilating her body."

Mike wrapped his arms around her and brought her into his warm embrace. Hutch was positive that the killer saw her in the victim's body. He more than likely knew the exact moment she was transported there. There was a shift in the energy surrounding them. The viciousness of the killings would escalate. He found a sick pleasure in mutilating this woman. She felt the rage and hatred that consumed him. Her skin crawled at the mere thought of this latest sadistic murder.

The image of the killer's cold eyes staring down at the victim filled her with fear. Her body still ached from the numerous stab wounds. The girl fighting back angered him and triggered the rage, but he now had the rush of inflicting pain on his victim so he would continue to seek it out.

Her head spun out of control as she tried to focus on his face once more. Pain wracked her body as she recalled the murder. His face was right in front of her, and she couldn't focus in on him.

Unable to take anymore, she walked into the bathroom and stripped. She studied her body thoroughly, searching for any signs that she had been stabbed. She had no marks on her breasts or stomach. There were no telltale marks, no fresh or tender wounds; yet she felt every stab he'd made. She assumed she would wake up to at least find her body covered in bruises or welts.

She sighed at her reflection in the mirror and turned away. She didn't want to dwell on the vision more than needed. The events that she witnessed were terrifying. She needed to take her mind off of the paranormal for a while. She would not let the increasingly gruesome visions take hold of her life.

She turned on the shower and let the hot water seep into her skin. She lathered with soap and washed the last of the fog from her vision down the drain with the soap. The memory was still fresh in her mind, but not as all consuming.

Chapter 46

The killer's eyes snapped open. The room was bathed in darkness with the exception of the red glow of his alarm clock. His breathing became rapid and fear caused his heart to pound furiously in his chest. He sat up and turned on the lamp by his bed.

He let out a sigh of relief as he surveyed the room. He feared the ghosts of his victims were watching him sleep once again. Relief washed over him as he confirmed that he was alone.

He got out of bed and went into his special room. After unlocking the door, he looked at his special possessions. They were all there.

He checked the top shelf to make sure her eyes were still there as well. The dark, gelatinous orbs bobbed in the filmy liquid. He let out a sigh of relief.

A voice whispered in his ear, "I knew you would check on me tonight. You can't stay away from me can you? You love me too much even now. You are such a pathetic excuse of a man!"

Her voice seared deep into his brain as he shouted at her, "Shut up!"

She moved closer to him, "My poor pitiful son, you will never be rid of me. Let me see what new trophies you obtained. I know you want to show them to your mother. Don't you want to hear how proud I am of you?"

"I don't need you anymore, Mother. There is nothing you can say that will make me want you in my life." He slammed the door shut and locked it.

He made sure that the door was secure before leaving the room. He chanted to himself, "She's dead now. She can't hurt you anymore." How was she able to talk to him after he removed her nagging tongue? He removed her eyes as well and yet she still saw everything he did, they all could. Maybe, he could be rid of her if he flushed them down the toilet. If only he could find the strength to dispose of them. Instead, he kept them securely locked away.

He passed by the dreaded closet, confirming that it remained boarded up. A shudder of fear snaked down his spine as he recalled the times he'd spent in that closet. She had enjoyed locking him in the darkness. She left him for days at a time in the darkness and peered at him through the narrow slot she had cut out in the door. Her dark evil eyes had stared at him through the opening. He grew to hate those eyes as they looked at him with disgust and loathing. He still remembered the maliciousness of her voice as she whispered through the slot in the door.

"Have the voices left you? Can you see them coming to you?"

He pled for her to let him out or to turn on the light, but her eyes just glared at him with hatred instead. Her footsteps echoed through the house as she left him alone once more. All he had were the ghosts that sought him out for companionship.

After several days, he broke down and swore he wouldn't talk to the spirits. The hunger that gnawed at his stomach or the burning thirst in his throat would become unbearable. He forsook his only friends for the necessities of life. When the loneliness became overwhelming, he started talking to the ghosts once again. He tried to keep it hidden from his mother, but she always knew when he welcomed them back into his life, as if she had some connection to them. She then punished him once more.

He refused to be put in that hellhole of a closet anymore. After his mother's death, he boarded up the small closet. He never wanted to worry about anyone ever locking him in that closet ever again. There was nothing but fear, despair and darkness to keep you company in that room.

The one thing he learned from his mother was patience. After all, it took patience to plan and wait for the opportune moment to kill. He laughed at the thought of his mother actually teaching him anything. That had never been her intent in life. Her cruelty, though, helped him become the man he was now.

He paced the floor of the old house as he tried to calm his emotions. Raw energy pulsed through his body and refused to let him go back to bed. Hatred and fear subsided as other emotions took over his body. It was time to hunt.

Chapter 47

Hutch looked up from her desk to find Detective Ledet watching her. "How in the hell did this guy go through life being a law abiding citizen then all of a sudden he is a serial killer?"

Hutch shook her head, "That's been bothering me too. I had a vision last night. I saw the jars in his special hiding place. There were more jars there than we have bodies. He has been doing this longer than we realize. For some unknown reason, he has become brazen and doesn't care if we find the bodies."

"How many jars did you see?"

"I keep playing the vision back in my mind, but the numbers change. There were at least ten pairs, but there may be more."

Ledet let out a long sigh, "Son of a bitch, why haven't we found those bodies?"

"I'm not sure. That may explain why I have been seeing so many ghosts. I thought the images of the women were distorted, but it may be they all tried to crowd into the vision."

"I will put another run through ViCAP. We have to be missing something. He may have killed in another small town and they never entered the data into ViCAP. It sure as hell makes it hard when we have no trail to follow."

As Hutch listened to Ledet speak, frustration dripped from every word he spoke. At least she was not the only one desperate to stop him.

Hutch's desk phone rang, and she knew another body had been found.

When Ledet, Bryant, and Hutch arrived at the scene, they were greeted with flashing strobe lights from the numerous police cruisers. Bryant replied, "It looks as if half the police force is here."

Hutch nodded her head in agreement. Ledet asked the young officer working the scene, "Who found her?"

"A fisherman going out this morning saw her car here and went to see if she needed help with getting down her kayak. He thought maybe she had a little trouble this morning since normally she was already out on the bayou. From what he said, the victim was here every morning. She mentioned to him before that she was training for a kayaking race on the bayou."

The detectives made their way across the uneven terrain to the crime scene. The coppery scent of blood and the odious smell of death hung heavy in the air. Dr. Ortego saw them coming and walked over to them. Bryant asked, "Does she match the same physical description as the others?"

Dr. Ortego replied, "She could be related to the last victim. They are similar in appearance. There was a lot more physical mutilation done to her body."

Hutch let out a long sigh, "He stabbed her over and over didn't he?"

Dr. Ortego replied, "Yes. She was killed and left here. He had a lot of rage for this victim."

Hutch nodded her head in agreement, "She fought back. Not only did it anger him, but it also excited him. I fear that any future victims will show the same amount of mutilation."

Dr. Ortego continued, "There is something else. We found a pair of panties stuffed in the neck wound."

A chill ran through Hutch. She didn't see that in her vision, "Was she sexually assaulted?"

"Not that I can tell. When we get her back to the morgue, I will do a thorough exam. She was dressed and wearing a pair of panties. I think the killer brought these with him."

Dr. Ortego handed Hutch an evidence bag containing the panties. She couldn't attest to it since they were covered with blood, but she informed him, "I think these are the underwear he stole from the house that night."

Ledet replied, "I don't like that he is making this case personal with you."

Hutch agreed, "I don't like it either. I haven't figured out how he knows I see him in my visions. He is peering directly at me now. He can find my exact location."

After they examined the body, the coroner's assistants prepared the body to be removed. As they loaded the body into the van, Hutch walked the crime scene. She tried to isolate herself from what happened around her. It was surreal to her how the sun continued to shine, and the birds continued to sing with this grisly murder having taken place right here. The world should stop for a few seconds and pay respect to the recently departed.

She heard the crime scene technicians and officers talking, but it was as if they were far away instead of right next to her. The mist took over her vision as she watched the killer appear. He walked the same trail that Hutch had just walked on. She called out to Rayne, "If you are near I could use your help. Maybe between the two of us, we can finally see him." She took a deep breath and centered her mind to concentrate. Slowly, the mist moved.

She saw the young woman as she got out of her car. The killer took her by surprise. She immediately fought back. The fear emitting from her was infectious. Hutch's heart pounded in her chest. She screamed and fought back with everything she had. He took her small figure for granted and was caught off guard by her strength.

As the girl continued to struggle with the killer, Hutch honed in on his face. She let out a sigh of disappointment. Once again, a plain white mask covered his face. It shined eerily in the early morning sky. The more she struggled, the more animated he became. Hatred poured from him as the woman fought back. The more she fought back, the angrier he became.

The young woman's sobs echoed along the bayou. Hutch knew what came next, and she wished she could block it from her sight. As the knife entered her body, it cut through the woman's skin as if it were butter. There was an explosion of blood all around them as the knife continued to be plunged into her flesh. Blood spurted and in some places gushed from the open wounds. A gurgling sound escaped her pale lips; the look of shock and terror frozen on her face.

Hutch tore her eyes away from the woman's body and stared at the killer. Even with the mask, she hoped to see something that led them to him. The killer's body shuddered with excitement at the carnage he'd just caused. He became overly aroused by the intense pain that he caused this fool of a woman.

Rage coursed through Hutch as she watched the killer. This woman did not deserve to die such a violent death. She did not deserve to have her life cut short. This evil being in front of her didn't deserve to walk this earth. She wanted to see him suffer for the torment, fear and pain he inflicted on these girls. She wished she had access to one of the soul collectors Joshua and Bianca used; she would unleash it on this monster.

As the vision dissipated, Hutch called out to Dr. Ortego, "She fought back. There may be DNA under her nails."

As Hutch came out of the vision, Ledet and Bryant were walking her way. Both men had been walking the perimeter of the scene. Ledet reached for his antacids, "You okay?" she asked.

"Yeah. These scenes are getting to me." Ledet looked over at Bryant, "What about you mon ami? Are these scenes getting to you yet?"

"Mon Dieu, these crimes are the biggest headache of my career yet."

As the two detectives talked, Hutch sensed a change in the air. There was a charge that wasn't here before. The killer was here, somewhere nearby. She scanned the crowd in search of any black figures hovering nearby, but she saw nothing but normal, everyday people for once. Did he let his true self show and she couldn't pick him out of the crowd? She called one of the crime scene techs over and asked, "Can you please take several pictures of the bystanders today? I don't want anyone missed."

"Yes, ma'am."

Chapter 48

He bolted upright in bed disoriented. A strange noise had awakened him. He cocked his ear and listened. Could it simply be ghosts haunting him at night once more? He heard the wind howling outside the windows. He had been in a deep, dreamless sleep before something woke him.

A woman appeared before the foot of his bed. It was not one of his normal ghosts who haunted him, nor was it Detective Hutcherson having another of her visions. No, this was someone new. His stomach tightened with a sickening feeling that only fear produced. The woman before him was the woman who helped Detective Hutcherson. He had heard whispers from the other ghosts that she offered her help to them.

He waited for her to say something, but she just stood there watching instead, "What do you want with me?"

A gust of wind rushed through the room and brought with it the coldness of death. A cold shiver ran through his body as the frigid air hit his heated skin.

She gave him a wicked grin, "I have been watching you."

He didn't like the idea of a ghost just sitting back and watching him, "What is it you watch me do?"

Her voice was calm yet cold as ice, "I know what you have done. They told me."

Hatred slithered through his body, coiling through like a snake, "You know nothing woman."

"I know you murdered those women. I know you have been killing for a while now. I have felt your evil lurking in the bayou. You have stabbed and mutilated. You ruined families by taking their loved ones away. Now, Grace has come to help me set them free. They want their eyes and tongues back. They want justice for the loss of their hopes and dreams. They will not rest until you are stopped."

He laughed at her, "You cannot stop me."

"You will be punished."

Spittle flew from his lips as he kicked back the covers to confront the ghost in front of him, "I will not be stopped. Grace, you or any of the ghosts condemned to this earth can't stop me. There is nothing you can do."

"We will be watching you. You cannot hide yourself from us forever. Soon, your mask will slip, and we will see who you are."

He ordered, "Get out of my room!"

The woman smiled coyly at him, "Just remember, we are always watching you."

He grabbed the knife he kept under the pillow and began to violently stab at the air. Rayne cackled at him. As she raised her arms and summoned up her powers, all the lights suddenly came on and exploded in the next instant. Satisfied that she'd caught his attention; she spun and captured the items in the room in her small tornado. When the wind died down, everything caught in her tornado crashed to the floor.

He surveyed the dark room. His heart pounded in his chest, his breathing became heavy, and his body drenched in a cold sweat. Ominous shadows danced across the room as darkness shrouded the corners making it impossible to see if she was coiled like a deadly snake waiting to strike once more.

He took in a few deep breaths to center himself. The energy in the room remained high, but not as highly charged as when she was there. She gave her warning and disappeared.

He dropped back down on the bed and looked at the alarm clock. It was two in the morning. The cold night air swept over his body. It did little to soothe the white hot anger coursing through his body. A vein throbbed in his neck. This woman had no idea who she was playing with. They were fools if they thought they could scare him this easily.

This ghost may think she could dissuade him with simple parlor tricks, but she was sadly mistaken if she thought parlor tricks would work on the likes of him. He refused to be anyone's puppet ever again. No one controlled him now and never would again.

Still, he was surprised that Detective Hutcherson had such strong powers for someone who claimed those powers just started. Could it be she misled everyone all along? How much could she do on her own and how much of this was being helped along by her ghost friend? Maybe it was time to send the ghost friend to the other side.

He could not fall back asleep even though the night was silent once again. He needed to think about what his next move would be. Detective Hutcherson would have to go, but not just yet. He was not done with her. He wanted to learn more about this connection she had with him.

Chapter 49

Ledet was dead on his feet as he walked into his house. Every step he took right now felt as if he had lead in his legs.

As he walked into the kitchen, he noticed that it was after midnight. He reached into the refrigerator and grabbed an ice cold beer. This was what he needed to wind down from the day he'd had.

While sitting at the bar and drinking his beer, his mind automatically wandered back to the case. These women's faces haunted him. This son of a bitch didn't leave them any evidence to follow. That bothered the hell out of Ledet. How could you kill so many women and not leave any trace evidence? This son of a bitch had to make a mistake soon; they always did.

He was getting more brazen and more vicious with each of his kills. The cooling off time in between the killings was getting shorter and shorter. The killings were closer together now. He would soon make a mistake, and when he did, Ledet would be there to slap the cuffs on him.

The next morning Ledet woke up feeling even more exhausted than when he went to bed. The inviting aroma of fresh blueberry muffins and coffee welcomed him into his favorite coffee shop. The blueberry muffins smelled too good not to try this morning.

When the waitress handed him his coffee and muffin, he smiled because both were nice and hot. He found a table near the back and reached into the bag for his treat. He slathered it with butter before biting into the tempting muffin. Sweetness and warm blueberry flavor burst into his mouth. He chewed slowly, savoring every bite. The complementary flavors of sweet berries and slightly salted butter somehow managed to put a smile on his face.

Just when Ledet thought his day had started to pick up, Bryant greeted him at the door. "The captain wants to see us in his office pronto."

Ledet had a sinking feeling in the pit of his stomach. If the captain wanted to see them in his office, it meant the powers that be had brought in the FBI. The captain was getting a lot of heat from the mayor's office to bring in the FBI, especially since this was a multi-jurisdictional case. The other city had no problem turning the case over to New Orleans. Hell, crime had been just as bad there. They didn't want or need another murder investigation. The public outcry and media coverage had been so intense that Ledet knew it was only a short time before the FBI would be brought in though.

Ledet was surprised to see a man dressed casually at the captain's desk. Whoever this man was he didn't look FBI, "Where is Detective Hutcherson?"

"She called this morning to say she was going to walk the crime scene one more time. Something still didn't sit right with her about the latest crime scene."

The captain just shook his head, "Well, I hoped that you would all be here for this impromptu meeting. Go ahead and shut the door so we can get started."

After the door was shut and everyone seated, Captain Ron Hensley made the proper introductions, "Detectives, I would like you to meet former FBI profiler Alex Hamilton. Alex this is Detectives Ledet and Bryant."

After greetings were made and hands shaken, they settled back down in their chairs, "Alex has come to offer his services in this case. The catch is he doesn't want anyone to know that he is here helping."

Alex went on to explain, "I was once a profiler with the FBI, but I have since started my own private consulting business."

Bryant looked him over, "Wait a minute, didn't you help solve several cases here in Louisiana and don't you write books about those cases?"

Alex nodded his head in agreement, "Something like that. I started writing true crime fiction to make the public aware of how these serial killers work and making them aware of the dangers. Most of the proceeds from sales go to the families of the victims. A trust has been set up for scholarships for the victims' children."

Ledet listened to what this profiler said, "Why is it you don't want your appearance here known?"

Alex replied, "Your captain has informed me that you are using a psychic. If the media discovers that I am working on this case, there is a strong possibility that they will get nosy about what is happening with this case. So far, you have managed to keep Detective Hutcherson's abilities out of the paper, but I fear with my appearance, it will be harder to hide her true nature. If the media knows I am here, they will question your every move; they will accuse the captain of doubting his team and calling in a profiler to help solve crimes. With the extra media attention, there is always a chance someone will talk."

Ledet shook his head, "I am sure Hutch will appreciate your concern. There are only a handful of us who know Hutch has certain 'gifts' shall we say; no one below Bryant and I know about her 'gift' and we plan on keeping it that way. That is also the way Hutch wants it. She fears that if the other officers discover she can see and talk to ghosts they will treat her differently and I agree. Cops tend to rely on gut instincts and not something they can't understand."

Alex asked, "And you don't mind working with a psychic?"

"After seeing what this monster did to those poor girls, I don't care if you claim aliens abducted you in the middle of the night. I am willing to listen to what you have to say. Especially, if you help me solve this case. You may be just what we need to solve this case. Hopefully, you can tell us what makes this guy tick."

Alex replied, "I must admit this is the first time I have worked with a psychic. I am skeptical about the whole thing. I always relied on physical data and analysis. I understand you have had several supernatural cases here lately, but I have a hard time wrapping my mind around it; however, I am willing to give this a try. The end result is that we all want to see this killer stopped."

Captain Hensley replied, "If it makes you feel better, we were all skeptical of this supernatural stuff at first. But after seeing it with your own eyes and working the cases, you become a fast believer. These cases helped broaden the scope of what we believe is possible."

"Well, I want to give you a basic rundown of what I came up with so far. I would like to review the files in more detail once we are done though."

Captain Hensley agreed, "Of course."

"Well, as you know, most serial killers here in the United States are male Caucasians in their mid to late twenties. They tend to suffer from antisocial personality disorder. The killer may appear to be charming on the outside. You are dealing with what the FBI refers to as a signature killer. He likes to leave a calling card if you will. Up until recently, the killer did not inflict any pain or suffering on the victim. That has all changed. I agree with Detective Ledet that this killer is escalating. He will continue to incorporate the same, if not more, amount of violence in his other kills. It gave him a high that he will continue to seek out. The fact that these women have similar physical characteristics means they remind him of someone in his life. It could be his mother or an ex-girlfriend, but a woman at some time in his past hurt him and hurt him bad.

"This guy kills for a specific reason. It isn't for sexual stimulation, and I don't see it being for monetary gain. There is a deep seated reason, but I am unsure what that is right now. I believe there may be another reason he takes the eyes and tongue, but the main reason is so he can keep track of his successes. There is a chance he takes them so he can reminisce about each kill. He could be showing someone his trophies to prove he recently killed. Just remember, my profile is still in its infancy, and I don't have a lot to give you. I hope that by this afternoon I will have more."

Ledet asked, "What if he took the eyes and tongue to his mother or significant other? Maybe, he wants to show her what he can do, and if she doesn't watch it, he will do the same thing to her."

"There is the chance that he already killed the person these women remind him of. However, he could be leading up to the moment when he kills the one these women represent. Something happened to him in his past that caused him so much pain and hatred that he is taking out the source of his pain, women. He may be like a lot of serial killers who do this for some warped sense of need. There is a chance he will eventually try to get caught. He may even try to arrange it so he is killed in the line of fire as he won't have the courage or strength to kill himself. He will consider this his punishment for the wrongs he has done."

Ledet's jaw clenched as he listened to what Alex Hamilton had to say. They could not wait until this killer's own debauched sense of justice kicked in. The killer knew this too, and that gave the killer an advantage. If only they had the manpower to protect every woman here in New Orleans.

When Ledet and Bryant got out of their meeting, they found Hutch in the conference room with several boxes of evidence sitting around her. Ledet asked, "What is going on?"

She looked up at him, "I decided to examine the personal effects of the victims. It's something I have never tried before, but if I touch them and concentrate perhaps I can pull some detail off of them."

Ledet informed her, "The captain brought in a profiler."

He saw her pale at the very word, "He brought in the FBI? Do they know about me?"

"Relax; he is a personal consultant and a skeptic. He isn't sure he even believes in your 'gift', but he is open."

"Well, hopefully, he has an idea on who this killer is because I sure don't. This guy keeps taunting me instead."

Ledet asked, "Where do you want to start then?"

"I will begin with the first victim. It would be nice if he left something of his behind besides the car tracks. If I could hold something of his, maybe it would help me get a clearer picture of him."

Hutch picked up a piece of clothing the first victim had worn, keeping it in the evidence bag she held it close to her. The poor young woman never had a chance to feel fear. She was dead before she even hit the ground. Hutch replied out loud to no one in particular, "This guy never hesitated when he killed her. It was one clean cut. She died almost instantly."

Ledet responded, "That is what Dr. Ortego said."

She asked, "If this were his first kill, then shouldn't there be hesitation marks? Even when he removed the eyes and tongue, he did it with surgical precision; there was no hesitation. He came prepared. He knew he would kill someone that night. He had the tiny jars with him."

She tried to concentrate on the killer more than the victim, but she could not change her focus. Frustrated she moved on to another victim's clothing. There had to be something here that helped them. Why couldn't she just look up from the victim's dead eyes and see the killer? If only she saw the killer with the same clarity as she saw the victims and the gruesome murders.

Hutch picked up the formal autopsy report and reviewed it; perhaps reading it would give her more insight into the killer. According to the report, there were multiple stab wounds and lacerations covering her face, neck, chest and abdominal region. There were a few slash marks on her arms, but those were noted as defense wounds. The young woman had fought back. Once again, there was not enough physical evidence to point out their killer's identity. There were almost ninety stab and slash wounds not including the slit to her throat and the removal of the eyes and the tongue.

Whoever did this was a sick bastard. In her opinion, knives were the most vicious form of weapon for murder; you had to be up close and personal with the victim. In some cases, you had to look the victim right in the eye as you killed them. Then you had to feel the knife as it pierced the skin and the blood as it ebbed from the body. This guy wasn't squeamish about blood.

Chapter 50

The familiar burning ache simmered deep inside of him. The need to hunt became overpowering. It was too soon after his last hunt; he shouldn't submit to it. He must stay in control. The need to kill had turned into an addiction; the desire for the exquisite physical release deep seated. The only way for this thirst to be quenched was to kill.

Unable to sleep, he took the taxi cab out. He found a young woman that looked perfect for him at the airport hailing a cab. A smile formed across his face. He couldn't believe his good fortune. This one may be just what he needed to tide him over for a while.

He helped her into the car, "Where to ma'am?"

"I have a reservation at the Chateau 'Orleans."

"That is a mighty nice hotel. It will take a few minutes to get there. Have a seat and enjoy the ride."

She smiled up at him, "Thanks. I hope I can keep my eyes open long enough to get to the hotel."

"You have nothing to worry about. I will wake you up when we get there. Just sit back and relax. The roads are fairly light at this hour."

***

Heather Guillory woke suddenly from a deep sleep. She waited for her vision to adjust to the darkness that surrounded her. Terror coursed through her like molten lava. She needed to remain calm and figure out where she was. Complete horror gripped her as she realized the taxi driver never brought her to the hotel. What the hell? An eerie silence surrounded her. She went to open the door and to her horror, she found there were no door handles or locks in the back seat.

In the faint moonlight, she saw a shadow coming towards the door. Someone was out there. "Please let me out." Fear quivered in her voice. There was still complete silence.

Her apprehension intensified. Her skin tingled with fear. "Please, you don't have to do this."

The door opened, and the taxi driver grabbed her. Terror had her paralyzed. What kind of game was he playing?

He grabbed her from the car and dropped her to the ground unceremoniously. He straddled her body and peered down at her through veiled eyes.

Oh dear lord, what did he have planned? Her mind raced with images of the vicious, vile things he could do to her. Fear reignited her attempts to escape; she struggled desperately against his weight. A dozen promises and resolutions ran off her lips as she bartered with God to save her miserable life. She vowed to change her ways and go on the straight and narrow if she lived.

A sneer formed on his face as she continued to fight him. Her stomach coiled in surprise as he wielded the knife over her head. She screamed in horror as he peered at her through dark, soulless eyes. She screamed so hard that her throat was raw and burning. Her heart beat so hard against her ribcage; she swore the bones would break.

White hot pain screamed through her body as the knife entered her body repeatedly. Her lungs were on fire. She struggled to gasp for air and prayed death came quickly.

She felt the strength leaving her body. She became extremely weak as blackness enveloped her. The pain was excruciating.

There was so much blood. She never imagined that much blood was in the human body. Surely, with losing this much blood, she should be dead. There would be no white knight in shining armor; no one came to her rescue. Death couldn't come quick enough. There were so many stab wounds on her body. Her tormentor was relentless. She felt the stickiness of the blood on her skin and the coppery smell it emitted.

***

The familiar thrum of excitement hummed inside of him like a high voltage electrical current. He sensed another presence teasing the periphery of his senses. A wicked smile formed across his face. Was it her? Was she here to watch? At first, he found it disturbing that an unknown entity watched his every move. "Stop watching me." He called out. "If you know what's good for you, you will leave now." Detective Grace Hutcherson was becoming a liability – one he couldn't afford to have.

He heard the voices echoing through his head; they must be silenced. He could no longer ignore the voices, but he must have fun first. If he killed her now, there would be no enjoyment?

With slow deliberation, he slid the knife's blade along her body. Too much time had passed since his last kill. The need clawed its way through his veins. He needed his fix just like a druggie. He took in a deep breath, not ready to lose control. He wanted to relish in the moment and to not rush it.

***

Hutch squatted down beside the body and replied, "This killing wasn't planned. It was a spontaneous kill. The hunger became too much for him. He is starting to lose control."

As Hutch read the energy around them, she sensed their killer was aroused and excited by this recent kill. She was nothing more than a spur of the moment kill and only brought him a quick release.

Chapter 51

As Hutch tried to force the vision to reappear, her body reacted to the impending terror with a shiver of premonition darting down her spine. Her body quivered as she forced herself to watch a sight she desperately wanted to escape.

Ledet watched as Hutch writhed in the chair as she relived the hellish vision. Her face was a mask of confusion that wavered between the fear that threatened to consume her and her own inner strength. She gripped the arms of her chair tightly and caused her knuckles to protrude through her tightening skin. He watched as Mike paced. It must be horrible to witness the violent attacks, but it had to be painful to watch as the woman you loved relived the visions repeatedly. This last attack was so violent that Hutch felt it would be better if she relived the vision in front of others just in case she missed something.

Her eyes and mouth opened wide in terror and for a moment, Ledet feared that she gave into that terror. Sweat beaded on top of her forehead as her eyes narrowed and stared into the vision. Her mouth moved in a silent expression; her breath barely made its way out. They waited impatiently for her to speak. "I'm not sure what I see. It's just images, shadows really."

Her skin paled as Hutch wove a story of fear, horror and pain well beyond anything Ledet could have ever imagined. As she spoke about the blind terror the victim felt and the rage the killer displayed, the air in the room changed. The fury the killer displayed was more than he had ever shown in the past.

Even though Hutch knew she was safe, the fear that filled the room consumed them. They all felt as helpless as the victims.

Mike took Hutch's hands in his, "Grace, listen to me. Look at him. Really look at him."

Tears spilled from her face. The scenario was exactly like the last. She gasped for air as the knife plunged into the victim's body repeatedly. Sweat beads formed on her forehead as she felt the pain, "He is viciously stabbing her. There is blood everywhere. Her screams echo throughout the night sky. She's losing consciousness." Mike felt Hutch's hands quiver underneath his, and he squeezed them a little harder. "I'm trying to get her to look up at him, but she keeps slipping back into the darkness. Wait, hold on, I see his face. He is wearing the same white mask once again. All I see is his cold, black eyes. There is only rage in them. I feel so cold when I look into his eyes. There is no joy inside of him."

Without warning, her head dropped heavily against her heaving chest. She took in a sharp intake of air, "I'm inside of him now. He's staring down at her; he is breathing hard. He gets up and heads back to his car."

Her body shook violently. The vision was coming to an end. She squinted hard trying to make out his car. "Wait, he's mumbling something. I can't tell what he is saying though."

Mike asked, "What is he saying Grace. Try to concentrate."

"His voice is too distorted. I can't hear it well. It's as if he is chanting."

Ledet told her, "Focus on the car."

"I'm trying to see the car, but the vision is fading." Her body tensed so hard Ledet thought it would lock her joints. Her teeth ground against one another. Her face seemed to distort in front of them; she became almost unrecognizable. Once more, she slumped into the chair. Mike handed her a bottle of water. She drank from it greedily. She was emotionally and physically drained. She wiped the tears from her eyes. She hated showing weakness in front of her fellow coworkers, but it was hard not to let the emotions take over your body when having such an intense vision.

Ledet plopped down on a chair in the room, trying to curtail the savagery that ate at his soul. He was angry at the lack of details once again.

These killings would continue to happen until they stopped him for good. They just couldn't do it with what they knew so far. It wasn't Hutch's fault, and he didn't want her to think she wasn't doing her part.

The silence in the room spoke volumes. It was several minutes before a word was said. Alex walked over to Hutch, "Can you do me a favor and tell me what you felt during this vision?"

She looked up at him in confusion, "What do you mean by what I felt?"

"I know there is something there. When you were inside his mind, you were on the verge of something. It was as if he knew you were inside of his mind and he tried to block you out."

Hutch shook her head, "I've tried to put a name to the feeling when I am inside of him, but I just can't define it. It is on the tip of my tongue, but I can't place it."

"What about the chanting?"

"It's as if he sees the ghosts and tries to get them to leave him alone. There is another presence there, one that terrifies him."

Alex informed them, "I am certain that he is killing the same person repeatedly. He uses these women by proxy. It is not uncommon for a serial killer to have a problem with their mother or another woman who played a significant role in his life."

Ledet agreed, "It's still too vague though. We can only speculate without more to go on."

Alex agreed. It wouldn't be long before the town was drenched in horror and blood if this killer was not caught.

Mike informed them, "I am going to get Hutch back home. She's exhausted and needs to rest."

***

As Alex watched them leave, he hoped Hutch could break through whatever barrier the killer put up that kept her from getting inside of his mind. He saw enough violent crimes to know that uncontrolled emotion, such as those displayed by this killer would cause him to make a mistake

sooner or later. The outcomes were usually never good.
Right now, they could only hope and pray it was sooner
rather than later.

Chapter 52

Ledet looked over at the alarm clock and was surprised to see that it was going on five o'clock in the morning. He couldn't remember the last time he'd slept past four. This case had been the only thing on his mind lately.

He walked into the kitchen and started the coffee pot before heading to the shower. After showering and getting dressed for the day, he walked outside to get the morning paper. He may as well enjoy a cup of coffee here and catch up on the news before heading into the office.

As he walked outside, he noticed the morning sky. There was still a hint of gray, bordering on purple, mixed with hints of pinks and oranges. If he stayed out a little while longer, he might witness an actual sunrise. But he didn't have time to linger, so he walked back into the house with the paper under his arm.

He poured himself a cup of coffee and settled at the kitchen table. He pulled the paper from its weather resistant bag and unfolded it in front of him.

The story on the front page caught his attention, and he saw red. He felt his blood pressure rising. There on the front page was a picture of Detective Grace Hutcherson as she walked the latest crime scene.

New Orleans Police Department Detective Claims to have a Psychic Link to Serial Killer

New Orleans, Louisiana – Murder bathes the bayous and streets of New Orleans once more with the blood of innocent young women. To date, local authorities won't comment for fear their investigations will be harmed. This serial killer has been terrorizing young women here in New Orleans for over eight months now, and police officials are still no closer to solving this crime.

A reliable source came forth stating that one of the detectives working on the case indeed claims that she has a psychic link to the killer. Even with her powerful link, they have very few leads, almost none to be exact. From what we have ascertained, the New Orleans Police Department is unable to gather any useful information on the case; therefore, leaving the detectives working on the case stumped and at their wits end. What is more disheartening is the fact that no one has asked the state or federal authorities for help. Pleas from the general public and the victims' families to find this killer seem to fall on deaf ears.

Ledet slammed his fists down on the table, "Son of a bitch!" He stood quickly and sent the chair crashing to the floor. Rage burned hot throughout his body. He looked for anything to turn his rage on but stopped himself before he punched a hole in the kitchen wall.

He took a few deep breaths until the red hot anger coursing through his veins smoldered to dying embers. When he felt calm and could trust himself not to punch the reporter in the face for not checking with him before publishing such nonsense, he picked up his keys and headed for his car.

Chapter 53

There was only one explanation for the sight in front of her this morning, bedlam. Phones rang continuously. People were shouting, muttering, swearing or rushing about. She heard fingers dancing across keyboards at alarming rates. The smell of fresh coffee was everywhere in the room. It was a typical morning at the New Orleans Chronicle. If you wanted to see chaos, you should be here at the deadline.

Chaos was a typical day for most of the staff, just like breathing. They were all involved in their own stories, paying no mind to what others around them were busy doing. It's not like they didn't have teamwork here, but they each had their own job to handle, and they handled it with expertise. They had the same obsession in this exclusive community, to get the story in before deadline. Each person here still greedily guarded their story, sources, and style. You had to thrive on pressure, handle confusion and know when you had a hot lead to be successful in this cutthroat business.

Melanie Wilson had always dreamed of being a reporter. She walked around with a notepad and pencil in her "briefcase" her mother made for her. She asked anyone who spoke to her various questions as if she were writing a story for the local newspaper. She worked almost every angle in this business. She worked in the mail room, carried coffee, ran copies, wrote obituaries and covered even the lamest of functions to have a chance to become a feature reporter.

She was born with the ability to smell a story and make the reader feel as if they were right there while it happened. Her father hoped she would take her skills and be a food critic, but that was not what she wanted. She took years of classes to hone her style and technique.

Now at the age of thirty, she was cynical. There was still a little humor left in her for life's twists and turns. She liked to be around people, but she saw what a person could do to another individual. She had grown restless in Atlanta, Georgia where there was always constant competition. She believed that she would never be good enough unless she exposed and exploited the human race to further recognition of her skills.

She left that rat race almost a year ago and greedily accepted the position as a crime journalist for the New Orleans Chronicle. She worked the police beat a few times in Atlanta and liked it. It was a tough world out there; murder and desperation were parts of it that couldn't be ignored. She didn't want just to write the story; she wanted the reader to feel the story.

The homicides she'd covered recently were senseless and cruel. These girls were an amusement to this killer. It took an extensive amount of effort to erase the images of each murdered victim from her mind, but at the end of the day, that was how she got through it.

When you first saw her, you wouldn't think she was a seasoned, hard boiled reporter but looks could be deceiving. At first, it exasperated her that people judged her on her looks, but now, she used it to her advantage.

***

Ledet looked down to see the culprit of his headache at her desk working on another article that might put one of his fellow officers in even more danger. He felt the anger building up inside of him once more and forced it back down.

He watched her for a moment. Her hair cascaded down her back in clouds of misty auburn. It was currently a curtain hiding her face. Her hair made a man want to dive in with his fingers and pull her closer to him. When she looked up to see him, he found himself staring into a pair of mesmerizing brown eyes with specks of gold. He imagined how they would look in the heat of passion.

She looked at Detective Ledet with piqued curiosity. Each of them snapped themselves out of their daydreams, "Detective, I am surprised to find you here. Is there something I can help you with?"

He was taken aback by her voice. It was pure heaven. It flowed like a leisurely stream; however, he found that voice just as deceptive as her angelic face. This lady must have an overly sharp, ambitious streak to report what she just reported.

As he slapped the newspaper article on her desk, she drew her brows together and asked, "What is this?"

His voice trembled with anger, "What is this? This article you wrote could be the death sentence for my detective. I want to know who your source at the station is, and I don't want to hear any crap about how that is privileged information."

She read the article he slammed down on her desk. She stood up without saying anything to him and headed off to the editor's office. He was right on her heels, "Don't you go running off on me."

She whipped around, not knowing he was that close behind her, and collided right into him. She looked up while poking her finger into his chest, "Listen here Detective Ledet, I have something that I need to take care of immediately. You can either follow me or sit at my desk until I have some answers." With each word she spoke, her voice increased. "I did NOT write this article; however, I did write an article similar to this, but this is not the article I wrote. Now, I need to find out what happened to my article."

She pushed her way into the editor's office without even knocking. She slammed the article on his desk, "Do you mind explaining what in the hell happened to my article?"

He held up his hands in defense, "I am trying to figure that out right now. My phone has been ringing off the hook. The New Orleans Police Department wants to know why in the hell I would even let one of my journalists print such rubbish." The editor of the paper looked at Detective Ledet and asked point blank, "This is rubbish isn't it Detective?"

"Of course the article is bullshit. I want a retraction printed immediately. The problem is, the damage has already been done. This one article could seriously put Detective Hutcherson in harm's way. I hope that the two of y'all are happy with the outcome of whatever in the hell game you are playing."

Both speaking at once, "Detective we are trying to find out just how this article got printed. This is not the article Melanie submitted."

Melanie glared over at Ledet, "This is not my article. I never even mentioned her in my article. I don't know how this happened, but I intend on finding out."

As Ledet listened to the two of them, a chill passed through his body. They suspected it could be someone who knew police procedure, and Hutch had a feeling that the killer was one of the bystanders. He barked out, "I need a list of your employees who have access to alter the article. I also need a list of those who have worked the crime scenes as soon as possible."

The editor cleared his throat, "Well, it appears that last night the website was hacked. The IT department is looking into this right now. They hope to have an answer soon. Trust me, we will find out what is going on. I don't like that someone can just come in through some back door and alter articles on a whim."

***

Melanie had never seen the man this up close and personal. He had a lean, well defined body that she felt was more at home in a pair of jeans than his slacks. His brown hair curled at the edges and made her want to run her hands through those curls right now.

As she watched the hunk of a detective storm off, her gut instincts told her that she would be hearing from him again in the very near future. Right now, though, she had more important things to take care of besides worrying about the very handsome Detective Ledet. She intended to find out who messed with her article. While she was at it, she planned on looking into this Detective Hutcherson. The good detective doth protest too much.

Chapter 54

Hutch heard someone calling out to her, but they sounded far away. Her eyes were heavy, refusing to open. The sleep her body craved, no needed, kept her just on the precipice.

Hutch felt someone pulling at her body. She felt them grip her shoulders, and her head snapped back. A searing pain ripped through her. Her throat was on fire. She felt as her body crumpled to the ground, and her life ebbed away. She woke up instantly only to find herself looking into cold, dark eyes. Her heart beat rapidly in her chest.

For the first time since her visions started, she could make out his hair. It was a dark brown, almost the same color as the victims. She saw the sweat bead across his forehead. She tried to focus in on his face. This was the first time she could make out any details on his face. With this one vision, she may stop this killer. She watched his jaw clench as he gripped her face. She couldn't think about what would happen to this poor woman. She had to concentrate on his face. *Come on Grace, you can do this. Don't think about what he is going to do. Take a good look at him. This may be someone you know.*

Before she could get a good look at his face, darkness closed in on her. Her last conscious thought was of his maniacal laughter echoing in her mind.

It was the cold that woke her up. It began at her toes and crept up her body along her nerves just before it seeped deep into her bones. Her eyelids fluttered as she slowly woke up from the cocoon of sleep.

Her eyes bolted open. She found herself submerged in the murky water of the bayou. The water moved in and out of the gaping knife wound on her neck. The tiny teeth and pinchers of small water creatures feasted on her torn flesh.

She bolted upright in bed and instantly grabbed her throat. As she relived the vision once more, there was something about the killer's eyes that kept nagging at her.

She reached for the glass of water she kept on her nightstand as she tried to recall his face. She could still feel the negative energy that surrounded him. This was the first time she came close to seeing his actual face.

Not wanting to wake Mike, she slipped out of the bed. She made her way through the dark apartment to the kitchen. Maybe a cup of coffee would clear her head so that she could concentrate on the face.

Hutch looked at the clock on the microwave and groaned. It was already five o'clock in the morning. There was no way she could go back to sleep. She would be waking in another hour to head to work.

After finishing her coffee, she decided she may as well take her shower. The freesia scented soap with the warmth of the hot spray helped calm her. She tried not to think about the murder, but the killer's face.

As she stepped out of the shower, her thoughts were still unsettled. As she looked at her reflection in the mirror, the face of the latest victim appeared. The hollowed out eyes caught her by surprise, and she instinctively jumped away from the reflection. She scolded herself for being so skittish. She couldn't afford to lose her focus now that she saw a glimpse of the killer.

She heard Mike waking up in the bedroom. She may as well make them a quick breakfast before they left for work since she was up and dressed.

***

Captain Ron Hensley waited for the task force to come in before sending them back out. The call came in just a few minutes ago. A poor fisherman went out early this morning to check his crab traps and returned with a poor catch, and the unfortunate experience of finding a body at the boat landing. Alex Hamilton was positive he left these bodies where they would be easily found to taunt them. He wanted to show them he could get away with murder, and they couldn't stop him.

He watched as they entered; the stress of the case was etched on each of their faces. Just about every one of them had a steaming cup of coffee in their hand. Some wouldn't even have a chance to enjoy their coffee before trashing it and heading out while others would try to gulp it down, needing the extra caffeine jolt.

They saw him at the door to the conference room and piled in. Their voices hadn't yet subsided as he closed the door, "We have another body."

***

Hutch watched as Captain Hensley gave them the particulars of the case. She was amazed at the lack of emotion he showed as he relayed the morbid details. The discovery of the dead body must explain the negative energy she saw hovering over him when she entered the precinct earlier. She also noticed that Bryant was slouched in his chair with his arms folded across his chest and his features showed impassive stoicism. Maybe she needed to learn from these two on how to keep her emotions hidden. She looked over at Ledet and saw the rage on his face. At least there was someone like her who showed his emotions.

Before sending them out, he stated, "You know the drill, process the scene and interview the man who found the body. Find out what time he arrived this morning. See if he noticed anything unusual. I know it was dark, but there is a chance the body was dropped off after he went out."

He looked over at Hutch to see if she could verify. She merely shrugged her shoulders. She had no idea if she had the vision at the same time as the victim's murder or not. "My vision was in the early morning hours, right around four o'clock, but I can't guarantee that was when he killed her. There are so many unknowns."

A misty fog surrounded the crime scene. The whole scene looked eerie with the sun dawning behind the dense canopy of trees and the fog slithering low to the ground through the trees. As Hutch climbed out of the car, she brushed off the remaining crumbs from her bagel.

A noise to the left of her caught her attention. As she headed to the area, she saw the spider web, shimmering with droplets of dew too late and walked right into its sticky path. Jumping back in disgust, she tried to remove as much of the web from her hair and clothes as possible. This day was not starting off well.

At the water's edge and away from the crime scene, was the apparition of the victim. For a moment, Hutch was afraid the ghost would disappear. She called out, "Wait. I didn't mean to scare you." Instead of fading away, the ghost just stood there looking at the crime scene. As if sensing that the apparition needed help, Rayne appeared. She took the young woman's hand in hers before looking over at Hutch, "You must be careful cher. I fear that danger is extremely near as of late. The killer is close I am positive."

Before Hutch could ask her any questions, Rayne and the victim's ghost disappeared. The air went unusually still. Hutch turned around quickly. She didn't see anyone but Ledet, Bryant, the crime scene techs and a few reporters that found out about the most recent discovery.

She reminded herself that she needed to pull it together. She had work to do, after all. Still, she surveyed the crowd once more hoping to see a black aura surrounding someone here at the scene. She was almost certain that the killer was here. There were so many areas for him to hide though that it would be impossible to search the whole area without more to go on.

Chapter 55

Ledet rubbed his aching eyes. He needed to make an appointment with the eye doctor. He'd strained his eyes so much over these last few months, his contacts weren't doing their job anymore. It was getting harder and harder to see the computer screen and forget about reading. He brought the papers up to his face to make out the words. He blamed the headaches on his poor vision, but that was not entirely true. This case gave him tension headaches. He felt it move from right between his shoulder blades up and through his skull. By the end of the day, it was almost more than he could take.

He let out a deep breath as he looked over the notes from Hutch's last vision. It was so eerie how she saw and felt what these unfortunate victims went through. Each kill seemed to be the same with the escalation of violence.

Now, she saw the killings through the killer's eyes, which was disheartening. If only she knew what the killer was saying. There was no doubt he was angered.

He knew that Alex felt this all went back to the killer's mother, but what if it didn't? What if Alex's Freudian theory was wrong about him hating his mother? The more Alex spoke, the more his theory did sound convincing.

At first, he was surprised Alex offered his help, especially for free. His original concerns were unjustified. It just went to show that gut instincts were not always correct.

They had to wait for the killer to make a mistake. Even the lab wasn't able to find anything useful. There were a couple of fibers under the latest victim's nails from run of the mill clothes, but that was not enough to go on. Their only hope was that Hutch would see something in more detail which could help them.

She could feel the rage building inside of him, and the room seemed to be charged with hatred as she talked about it. With that much rage, he would make a mistake soon.

He stared into the night. Was their killer out there right now hunting? Would they get a call saying another body had been found or would Hutch call to say she had yet another gruesome vision? He felt a twinge of guilt move through him just thinking about it.

It was getting difficult to tell the victim's loved ones of their untimely deaths. As selfish as it may sound, he wasn't sure if he could do it again. It took a little piece of his soul every time. He had reached his limits and couldn't stand to face another pair of sorrowful eyes as they waited for the news.

Chapter 56

As Ledet walked into the police station, he reached for his antacids. He didn't know how his partner did it. His stomach was killing him. This case had him tied up in knots. Maybe, if he could keep his emotions out of it, they would solve this case. His head was hurting so bad that he felt as if it would explode at any moment.

He walked over to the receptionist. "Brenda, you don't happen to have any ibuprofen do you?"

As she dug through her purse, she asked, "What's wrong? You got another headache?"

"No, I thought it would be fun to watch you go through that monstrosity of a thing you all call a purse."

As she handed him the medicine, she snapped, "You don't have to be such an ass about it."

He felt like such a heel. He rubbed his temples in an effort to relieve his headache. "I'm so sorry. You are right. I shouldn't take it out on you. I'm irritable and don't feel well. My head feels as if a marching band is inside of it."

She looked at him sympathetically, "Why don't you do like your partner? You have all been burning the candle at both ends and deserve a few hours to yourself."

"Bryant left?"

"He left a few minutes ago."

As Ledet poured himself a cup of coffee, he wondered why Bryant didn't tell him he was leaving early. He looked at the ibuprofen before washing them down with the coffee. He winced as the bitter coffee hit his already aggravated stomach.

He sat down at his desk and took his phone off the hook. He also turned his cell phone on quiet. He needed a few minutes of peace and quiet. He had to stop his mind from its frantic racing and rest.

He leaned back in his chair and waited for the ibuprofen to kick in. Even though he was trying to force his mind to stop thinking about the case, it automatically went back there.

He picked up his phone and slammed it back on the base. This wasn't getting him anywhere. Even when he tried to rest, his mind wandered right back to the case, as if it was on autopilot. He opened the file and reviewed the information once again. He must stay focused. It still bothered him that their killer was suddenly wearing a mask in the visions that Hutch was having. Could there be more to it than he didn't want her to see his face? What if it was because she knew him? What if that was why there was such a close connection there?

Alex Hamilton knocked on his door, "Everything okay?"

"What are you still doing here? I figured you would have gone back to your hotel room."

Alex shook his head, "Something just isn't sitting right with me about this case. The fact that this killer is masking his face in Hutch's visions has me concerned. If this was a total stranger, why would he care? Even if she could describe him to a sketch artist, we would still have to find him. No, there is more to it than that."

Ledet stared at the pictures up on the murder board, "I am missing something I know it. He killed some and literally left them where they dropped, but others he dumped in the water. We know Hutch saw more jars than we have bodies, so there are more bodies out there. Some of these women have been stalked while others were killed spontaneously. What does this all mean?"

Alex informed him, "I have a theory. What if he killed and left those at the scene because he knew there was no trace evidence? Those left in the water was because he feared there was some trace evidence that he needed washed away. We also know he has started to lose control. He's not as cautious as he once was. There is a chance that some victims will never be found. Maybe he doesn't want those bodies found. Maybe, something went wrong, and he wasn't sure if he left trace evidence on them; evidence he knew he couldn't erase without bringing more questions."

Ledet drew in a sharp breath, "You think he is a cop don't you?"

"I haven't ruled it out; it has me wondering because Hutch saw the taxi signs, but this guy is overconfident. It is as if he sees himself as invincible; however, I think he is finding it difficult to control the hunger growing inside of him. I also believe he blames Hutch for these feelings. His killings are becoming more frequent. He needs constant gratification. The satisfaction of the kill isn't lasting long anymore."

Ledet's voice grew bitter, "To tell you the truth, I suspected a cop earlier, but I ignored my gut instinct."

"I just keep thinking about how he killed mostly from behind. He knew to not leave any trace evidence and even when he viciously murdered these last women, there still was no trace evidence. There should at least be something under their nails, but it was almost as if he took the time to clean up after himself. The other possibility was that we could be looking at a forensics specialist or someone who works in the coroner's office. Hell, it could be anyone who has knowledge of how these cases work."

Ledet scratched his head, "The problem is nowadays everyone knows about forensics, but I have a feeling you are right. We need to look at someone with personal knowledge of the law enforcement field."

Ledet felt sick. He went over in his mind what Hutch had said about the killer's house.   Something had been nagging him since she described it. He jumped up from his desk, "I know who the killer is and Detective Hutcherson is in grave danger if I am right."

Why in the hell didn't he see it before? The killer had been right in front of their eyes the whole time. He felt like such a fool. The lack of emotion that he showed on cases should have been an indicator that something wasn't right. Now, he had a head start on them.

Picking up his phone, he called Detective Hutcherson. He exclaimed out loud, "Shit, she isn't answering her phone. That isn't like her."

Next, he dialed Mike's phone, "Is Hutch with you?"

Mike informed him, "No, she went home. I got called out on a case right as we were leaving."

"Do me a favor. If you hear from her, please have her call me as soon as possible."

"Yeah, I can do that, but if she isn't answering her phone, leave her a message. She may be in the shower."

Ledet didn't tell Mike about his suspicions right then. There was no sense worrying the man if he was wrong. He gave his cell phone to Alex. "Keep trying Grace, please."

Alex hit redial while he felt the power of the Dodge Charger kick in and the scenery became one long, continuous blur.

Alex prayed that they arrived in time.

Chapter 57

Detective Grace Hutcherson had just made it home when she heard the knock at the door. She looked through the peephole and was surprised to see him at her door. "I'm surprised to see you here this late. What can I do for you?"

A chill went down her spine as the blood in her veins turned to ice. When he looked at her with those cold, dead eyes, she realized her mistake. This man in front of her did not resemble the man she knew. She tried to slam the door shut, but he was too quick.

As he pushed her into the house, he locked the door. His voice was at a fevered pitch, angry and out of control. "You are turning into a problem cher. I didn't think anyone would buy that psychic mumbo jumbo, but they did. I should have paid closer attention to you when you first appeared, but I didn't think your abilities were as great as they are. You have become a wrinkle in my plan. Sooner or later you would have seen my true identity in one of your visions, and I can't have that."

Hutch found herself paralyzed with terror as she listened to him talk. She pushed herself hard against the wall, hoping to blend in. How she wished she could rush running and screaming out the door. The only thing hindering her was him.

She tried to keep her voice calm as she spoke to him, "I'm sorry you felt that I was becoming a hindrance. I had no idea who you were until you stared at me just now. We have known each other all this time and I never once knew."

He laughed at her, "I made sure to never allow you to touch me. As your powers strengthened and you were learning to hone in your control, I knew if you ever touched me, you would see my inner self. I have been wearing charms and Gris Gris bags to help keep my aura hidden from you. Now, I find myself in a very peculiar predicament."

Hutch calmly stated, "Mike will be home soon."

He let out a maniacal laugh, "You fool. You didn't think I would take care of him first. Mais non, he will be tied up for hours working a case that they believe is vampire related."

So, that's why Mike called to tell her he would be late. He was in a rush to give her too many details. Hutch asked, "So, you can speak with the dead as well?"

He sneered at her, "As a child, my mother treated me as if I was a freak of nature. When I was little, I sat in the corner for hours and had conversations with the wall. I told her once who I was talking to, and she locked me in a dark closet. From that point on, I tried not to talk to them while she was around because whenever she caught me it was right back into the closet I went. I thought by cutting out her eyes and tongue, she could no longer haunt me, but she kept coming back in other bodies. Everywhere I look, I see her face. The voices won't stop taunting me." He let out another sinister laugh, "I fixed her good though. After I had killed her, I boarded up that old closet she had locked me in. Mais non, no one will put me in that place ever again. Now, you have forced me to move on, but before I do, I must make sure you are silenced."

Fear took over, and Hutch pushed it aside. Now was not the time to let him sense that she was afraid. She drew in several deep breaths. She was afraid to close her eyes right now; she was unsure if she would see her death before it happened. Would her death be quick or would he make her suffer? Did he plan on keeping her tongue and eyes in a jar as well? She pushed those thoughts out of her mind. She couldn't think like that. She had to focus on protecting herself and finding a way out of this situation.

If she screamed, would anyone in the apartment complex hear her and if they did, would they even bother to call the police? She had to keep him talking. He couldn't kill her if they were talking, right?

A smirk formed on his face and his features turned cruel and harsh. His voice became deadly. "You should be terrified of me, you know. I am better than you."

She asked, "How was I a threat to you? I never even knew your true identity." As she talked, she slowly backed away from him.

"You have been a pain in my ass from the very get go. I read it in the cards that you were close to seeing my true identity. I couldn't let that happen."

She replied, "Yet, there are so many ways to read the cards, and they may have been wrong as well."

"No, I have seen the future. I have seen you finding my true identify and locking me away. I can't go back to a cold, dark room. I will not be locked up again. No, you are causing me too many problems and headaches. The media focused on the victims and not me, thanks to you."

He was babbling now. Hutch saw his aura changing before her. He was rapidly losing control. His voice turned into pure evil. His maniacal laughter echoed through the house. It sounded like an animal's howl and sent a chill of terror down her spine. There was a hateful edge to his tone.

In her mind's eye, she saw him drawing the knife out of its protective sheath, and she took another step back in preparation to make a run for it. Her only chance may be to lock herself in the bedroom and climb down the fire escape. Except he was blocking her escape route.

Before she could react, she saw him lunge. Pain seared through her right side. She stumbled backwards, but she managed to keep her balance. If she fell, he would be on top of her in an instant. At least, for now, she had a chance to make a run for it. Her hand moved to her right side. The warm blood flowed between her fingers at an alarming rate.

Hutch felt herself going limp. Her legs could barely support her. He kept advancing. She was slipping into the darkness. She shook her head, trying to keep him in her sights.

As they danced back and forth, he tried to stab her again. Even in extreme pain and bleeding like a stuck pig, she was once again quick on her feet. Suddenly, voices filled the air. Dark shadows moved in, taking shape. Hazy images of his victims appeared. Her brain tried to focus in on him once more, but she was afraid that if she took her eyes off of him just for a second he would attack.

***

Detectives Mike Bailey and Guy Mayon were inspecting the body as they waited for Dr. Ortego to arrive when Mike felt a frigid burst of air blow past him. He turned to Guy, "Did you feel that?"

Guy rubbed his hands over his arms, "Yeah, a cold breeze just blew across the scene. It was weird. We have been listening to Hutch's stories a little too closely."

Mike caught a scent of the bayou next to him even though they were in an alleyway near the French Quarter. Mike heard a woman whisper in his ear, "You must go to her before it is too late." He looked around to see who was there. Not seeing anyone, a sense of foreboding took over his body. The voice shouted louder in his ear, "Go now!"

Before he could respond, the night air was filled with an ominous voice shouting, "GO!"

It stopped everyone in their tracks. He saw the bewilderment in Guy's eyes. Mike told his friend, "We have to go now. Grace is in trouble."

"Mike, what was that?"

Mike was already concerned when Ledet called and now this. "I think that was one of the ghosts Grace talked to us about. She was warning us that Grace is in serious trouble."

As Mike left, he called the dispatcher, "Send an ambulance, SWAT and whatever you have to my house. There is an intruder there."

As he drove back to their apartment, Mike gave the dispatcher the relevant information. Mike and Guy both tried to call Grace's cell phone with no luck. It just rang. Mike told Guy, "That's not good. Grace wouldn't just ignore her phone."

As they made their way to the apartment, numerous questions ran through Mike's mind. What made this killer want Hutch so bad? Why try to kill her now? Was she getting too close to something, and she didn't even know it?

He placed the light on the top of his car and disobeyed all traffic laws. The engine quickly reached one hundred forty mph as he rushed home. He pushed the car to its limits praying he arrived in time. Cold fear constricted Mike's heart. He worked hard to keep a clear head, but visions of the victims flashed through his mind.

Guy didn't' even bother to talk to Mike. There was no sense in distracting him while they were traveling at such a high speed. Neither had any desire to be wrapped around a tree. At this rate of speed, it would not be a pretty sight.

***

Hutch found the darkness enveloping her. There was no chance of survival now. At any moment, he would plunge the knife into her body once more.

As she crumpled to the floor, the door crashed open, and a gunshot rocked the room. The sound of a body thudding hard against the floor followed the gunshot. Hutch's last conscious thought was how she would never see Mike's face again. Time had stopped, and silence filled the air.

Detective Ledet went over to Hutch as Alex Hamilton made his way over to their killer. He kicked the knife far from the body as he checked for a pulse.

Detective Ledet called for the First Responders waiting outside "Get the medics in here now. She has a faint pulse, but it is unsteady."

Alex shook his head, "It was a good kill shot. He's gone."

Mike pushed everyone out of the way and took Hutch's hand in his. It was already turning cold to the touch. He called out to her, "Grace…. Grace…. Grace please don't leave me. Get those medics in here now."

***

Hutch heard someone calling out to her. There was darkness all around her. It was so cold. Suddenly, she was surrounded by a warm light. She saw shadows moving towards her. It was those that he killed, and they were all around her. She felt their peace envelop her. She knew she was dying. There was no pain, just a welcoming peacefulness.

The First Responder gently moved Mike out of the way, "Sir, you have to let us in. Please!"

The medic shouted to his partner, "We are losing her. Let's go. Call the hospital and let them know we have a police officer coding from a knife wound."

***

Mike felt the ground underneath him opening up as he heard that Hutch was coding. If only he had arrived sooner. He picked up his phone and called Father Trahan, "I need your prayers. They are rushing Grace to the hospital. She coded. There was so much blood."

Guy took the keys from Mike. "Come on mon ami. I will take you to the hospital. You are in no shape to drive."

He felt as if he was in someone else's body as he was led to the car and they made their way to the hospital.

Chapter 58

A continuous beep echoed through her head. She reached out to hit Mike and ask him to turn off the blasted alarm clock. Why wouldn't it stop that incessant beeping? She couldn't move her arms; they were heavy. When she went to roll over on her side, an excruciating pain shot through her midsection.

She tried to open her eyes, but they were too heavy. In the distance, she heard someone calling her name, "Grace… Grace… Come on honey. Open your eyes for me just once my love."

Another voice, a female voice, was talking, "I gave her something for the pain. She should feel better soon."

She attempted to open her eyes once more but found herself slipping back into the darkness. She tried to remember what happened, but her mind was fuzzy. She was just so very tired. She drifted back to sleep.

When she woke up again, she remembered the pain and didn't move. She cleared her throat and tried to speak.

Mike was standing above her with worry etched on his face. He looked as if he hadn't showered or shaved in days. She went to say something again, but he placed a finger over her mouth, "Don't talk just yet. Let me give you some ice chips first."

She welcomed the cold wetness from the ice. It felt good as it went down her irritated throat. She watched as a rush of emotions washed over Mike's face. He gently stroked her hair. There was no need for words. Their feelings were so strong that no words could express as beautifully what their silence said.

She barely whispered, "What happened?"

Mike asked, "Do you remember anything?"

Hutch shook her head, "No."

"You are in the hospital. You had surgery to repair the damage made by the knife wound. It was touch and go for a while." He let out a deep sigh, "Oh, my love, I thought I lost you forever."

Hutch closed her eyes as bits and pieces of images flooded her mind. "Did you catch him?" she croaked out.

"You don't remember?"

She gently shook her head. The movement sent excruciating pain throughout her body, "Detective Ledet and Alex Hamilton figured out who the killer was. It came together as they recalled one of your visions. Ledet drove Bryant home one night after he'd put away a few drinks too many. The place was overgrown. Ledet made it to our apartment just as Bryant was getting ready to stab you again. Thankfully, I had already called for backup and an ambulance. They were already dispatched to our apartment when Ledet arrived."

She asked, "He's dead?"

"Yes. Ledet shot him right between the eyes."

"Wait, why were you on the way to the apartment? You were working a case."

"You can thank Rayne for that. She sensed you were in trouble and called out to me to help you. I don't think Guy will ever allow me to drive again."

The nightmare was over. No more girls would die at his hands. She heard a commotion at the door. Mike informed her, "You have several people here to see you."

He waved his hand for them to come in. Tears filled her eyes as her parents entered; they both looked as if they had been crying for days. Her mom came over and squeezed her hand, "How are you honey?"

"I am so glad to see you Mom and Dad." Hutch felt sleep pulling her under once more, but this time she could sleep without the visions haunting her every dream.

Ledet walked into the small hospital room and looked down at the sleeping patient, "I had hoped to catch her while she was awake, but I will let you tell her all in good time. Forensics just finished processing Bryant's house. He had 15 sets of eyes and tongues in his special closet. They have been sent to the lab for analysis to confirm which ones belong to which bodies. I don't think we will ever find all the bodies they belong to."

***

The woman watched from the corner of the room as Hutch fell asleep. She felt a peace wash over her. Could this be the one who would help her find the way back home? She had been trapped in these walls for far too long; they all had. After all of these years, no one was able to help them, but maybe, just maybe, they had found their savior. Someone must be warned because evil walked these halls once more. Their numbers were growing, and would continue until he was stopped.

Chapter 59

Mike paced back and forth in the apartment waiting for Hutch to finish dressing. When he walked into the apartment that fateful night and saw her lying motionless in her own blood with her lips parted, he realized that he couldn't live without her. He clung to the softness of her body in that hospital bed because he needed her strength as well as her. That was when he knew that just living together wasn't enough for him.

***

Hutch paused by the bedroom door, watching Mike pace. She wondered what he was up to. He had been acting strange all day. He acted nervous about going out to supper tonight, even though Beazell's On the Bayou was their favorite restaurant.

Hutch was just as nervous. She decided to tell Mike about her plans for the future. After almost being killed, she changed her perspective on life. She hoped he could accept what she must do. She found some peace knowing that those who were murdered by Bryant finally moved on. If only she could help Rayne move on.

He saw her in the doorway and smiled over at her. He walked over to her, sweeping her into his arms and kissed her before asking, "Are you ready?"

She held out her hand, "Let's go get something to eat. I am famished. I don't understand why you wanted us to get all dressed up though."

"It's been a long few months, and I thought we could use some time as lovers and not cops."

She stood up on her tip toes and kissed him once more, "You are so right."

As soon as they entered the restaurant, the maître d' walked right over to them, "We have your table ready sir."

Hutch figured they would sit at their usual table, so she was surprised to see that they were being led to a small private dining room. She gasped in surprise. It was such a romantic setting. There were red, pink and white roses throughout the room that was lit only by candlelight. Romantic music played in the background. It sounded as if a small orchestra was in the room with them. She smiled up at Mike, "You did this?"

He smiled as he heard Mr. and Mrs. Beazell walk into the room, "With a little help from our good friends."

Hutch walked over to them and gave them each a huge hug, "Are you joining us for supper?"

Mr. Beazell shook his head, "Mais non, cher. This is for y'all. We just wanted to make sure everything is to your liking."

Mike patted his buddy on the back, "Thank you so much for this mon ami and you too, cher."

After they had said their goodbyes, Mike pulled out Hutch's chair and waited for her to take a seat. "Oh Mike, this is so romantic. I wish I knew you had this planned." As Hutch looked around, she hated to talk to Mike about the changes she wanted to make for her future; maybe, she should just wait until tomorrow and enjoy tonight.

As they were talking, the waiter brought each of them a cocktail. It was Hutch's favorite, a Bloody Mary garnished with a jumbo boiled shrimp, pickled okra, pickled green beans, celery and garlic stuffed olives. He set their oysters on the half shell appetizer with accompaniments on the table as well.

Hutch looked at Mike in confusion. He smiled over at her, "I asked them to prepare a special meal for us."

Instead of complaining, she picked up an oyster, sprinkled it with some of Beazell's House Seasoning and a dash of hot sauce before letting the luscious oyster slide down her throat. The fresh oysters were irresistible with the perfect salty, briny taste.

Just as they were finishing the appetizer course, the waiter brought in their first course. Hutch's mouth watered as the tantalizing smell of the barbecue shrimp served on butter lettuce with spicy dipping sauce and the French baguette toast reached her nose. She moaned in sheer ecstasy as the barbecue shrimp flavors danced across her tongue.

As they dined on the first course, Mike and Hutch made general conversation about their day. It wasn't long before the waiter came back to take away the first course dishes and brought out the main entrée.

She smiled over at him, "I may let you do all my ordering from now on. This is an exquisite meal."

Mike reached over and squeezed her hand, "After the ordeal you went through, you deserve to be pampered."

As Hutch looked over the main course, she wasn't sure what she wanted to dive into first. There was pan seared salmon topped with an Atchafalaya lump crab sauce. There was also bacon wrapped asparagus, sautéed baby carrots and herb butter.

With a sultry smile, she told Mike, "You know I will have to work off these calories don't you?"

He gave her a smile that sent molten lava through her veins, "Damn, you found out my ulterior motive behind this meal."

Hutch was in heaven over the exquisitely prepared salmon. It was seasoned and cooked to perfection. The salmon was tender and flaked beautifully with just the touch of her fork. It was a good thing she ran as much as she did because eating here as often as she did could put a few inches on her waistline. She took one of the delicate asparagus spears and cut it in half with her fork.

The owners took pride in the quality of food they served. Everything was fresh. They also made heavy use of local fishermen, area farms and producers for the creative yet approachable menus. Grace believed in supporting the local businesses.

She smiled in pleasure as the dessert was served. It was a decadent double chocolate bread pudding with bourbon sauce, garnished with fresh raspberries and mint. This was pure chocolate heaven. This dessert was one fit for the gods.

After they had finished eating, Mike stood up, extended his hand to Grace and said, "Would you care to dance?"

She nodded her yes and fell into his arms; she never once missed a chance to have those strong arms of his wrapped around her. Being in his arms was heaven. His warm embrace sent a mixture of excitement and contentment flowing through her body. They moved gracefully across the floor. She felt like a fairytale princess.

He pulled her close to him and kissed her. His tongue slipped inside her mouth. His lips were silk against hers. His kiss ignited something deep inside of her.

There was a bottle of champagne and strawberries waiting at the table for them. What caught her eye was a tiny black box next to the champagne bottle.

She watched in utter surprise as Mike came over to her on bended knee. Tears glistened in her eyes, "Grace, almost losing you the other day made me realize that I don't want to continue just to live with you. I want to be with you for the rest of my life. My life is nothing without you. You have my heart in your hands. I will cherish you always."

She bent down and kissed Mike as dread moved into her heart, "Mike, I love you with all my heart. I would love to be your wife. I wanted to talk about this tomorrow, but maybe you should hear me out before you decide if you want to ask me to marry you."

She took a sip of champagne before telling him what she needed to, "I don't want to continue with my career full time. I enjoy it thoroughly and love the fact that I can work with you, but after almost dying, I realize I want more from life. I have received a few requests from other agencies wondering if I could help them with some cold cases." She took his hands in hers, "Mike, I have decided to leave the police force."

The news astounded Mike. He did not expect that, "Are you certain this is what you want to do?"

“Yes, I am sure.”

He informed her, “Guy and I were planning on talking to you as well. Guy is tired of the police force. He wants to re-open his detective agency and wants us to join him. He has received a few calls from parents with missing children requesting his help. He was good at what he did and if we can bring you into the business with your ‘gift’, we may have a better chance of solving these cases.”

“Let’s do it then Mike.”

Mike held her face as he kissed her. She had such a beautiful face, especially when love was spread all over it. He took a moment to look at her, “Grace, you my love, have an amazing heart. I am continually blown away by the love you share with me, your family and anyone who is lucky enough to be close to you. I would be honored to share my life with you.”

“Yes, Mike, I will be your wife. There is one thing you should know, I eventually want a baby.”

“I can’t think of anything I would love more than giving you a child.”

He kissed her with an all-consuming kiss that touched her very soul. Her emotions spilled out more empathetically than she anticipated. It soon built to a very passionate crescendo. Realizing where they were, they broke away from the kiss. He picked up the ring and slipped it onto her finger. With tears in her eyes, she kissed him once more.